To Karen-
xo
Heather Slade

TACKLE

K19 SECURITY SOLUTIONS

BOOK NINE

USA TODAY BESTSELLING AUTHOR

HEATHER SLADE

TACKLE

Paperback: 978-1-953626-05-9

MORE FROM AUTHOR HEATHER SLADE

BUTLER RANCH

Kade's Worth

Brodie

Maddox

Naughton

Mercer

Kade

Christmas at Butler Ranch

WICKED WINEMAKERS' BALL

Coming soon:

Brix

Ridge

Press

K19 SECURITY SOLUTIONS

Razor

Gunner

Mistletoe

Mantis

Dutch

Striker

Monk

Halo

Tackle

Onyx

K19 SHADOW OPERATIONS

Code Name: Ranger

Coming soon:

Code Name: Diesel

Code Name: Wasp

Code Name: Cowboy

THE ROYAL AGENTS OF MI6

The Duke and the Assassin

The Lord and the Spy

The Commoner and the Correspondent

The Rancher and the Lady

THE INVINCIBLES

Decked

Undercover Agent

Edged

Grinded

Riled

Handled

Smoked

Bucked

Irished

Sainted

Coming soon:

Hammered

Ripped

COWBOYS OF CRESTED BUTTE

A Cowboy Falls

A Cowboy's Dance

A Cowboy's Kiss

A Cowboy Stays

A Cowboy Wins

Table of Contents

Prologue

Tackle

Six in the morning, and I was out wandering the streets of Boston's Little Italy, looking for a woman who didn't want me to find her. I walked past the closed-up shops and restaurants that dotted the first floor of buildings now labeled "live-work spaces" although I doubted a single business owner in this area lived in the luxury apartments above them.

There were worse neighborhoods where Sloane could've chosen to hide out. If, in fact, she was here. It was certainly understandable why it would've appealed to her. Mass General Hospital was within a mile's walking distance, and her office was even closer. Not that she was going into work very much these days.

She'd done a damn good job of disappearing in the couple of days I was gone, called away to take care of something I wanted no part of.

I hadn't seen or heard from her since the day I left the house I had been painstakingly renovating for us to live in. If she'd have me, which now remained to be seen.

When I said goodbye that morning, I had no inkling that when I returned, I'd find out she'd ghosted me.

"Sloane, where the hell are you?" I muttered out loud, scanning the high-rises as if she'd come out on the balcony of one and I'd spot her.

"You're too early if you're looking for Sloane," said a kid sweeping the sidewalk in front of a coffeehouse.

"You know somebody by that name?"

"Really pretty, stomach out to here?" The kid, who couldn't be more than ten or eleven, held his hand out in front of him.

Rather than respond, I took the photo I'd brought with me out of my pocket. "This her?" I asked, handing it to him.

"Yep. That's Sloane."

"Have you seen her?"

"I did the last two days."

"Where?"

"Here," the kid said, laughing as he swept dirt onto the street. "Comes down for breakfast, but not until later."

"What time?"

He shrugged. "Not before nine or ten, after the morning rush is over."

"You said she comes downstairs. Does she live in this building?"

"Anthony!" a man yelled.

"I gotta go. See ya, mister."

"Hey, wait!" I was too late. The kid was inside with the door closed behind him.

1

Tackle
Previous November

I raised my head and surveyed the sterile room I was in. The smell was as familiar as the surroundings; I was in a hospital.

The last thing I remembered was lying on the floor of an airplane that was about to crash-land. I said a prayer, more for my family than myself, but the last image I saw was the same one haunting me now when I closed my eyes—Sloane Clarkson—my best friend's younger sister.

As hard as I tried to shake her from my thoughts, she always rose to the surface of my consciousness. She invaded my subconscious too, appearing regularly in my dreams. Sloane, who I'd watched grow from a gangling eleven-year-old to the most beautiful woman I'd ever laid eyes on, became my ultimate fantasy.

What little she and I had experienced in reality, morphed into scenes merged with dreams I'd had of her. Ones in which a simple hug hello ended with her sprawled naked on a bed. It could be any bed; I was unaware of anything in the room other than it and her.

"*Buenos días,*" said a woman dressed in scrubs as she walked into my room. "*Señor* Sorenson."

"*Buenos días.*"

She took my temperature, checked my blood pressure, and listened to my heart.

"Where am I?" I asked.

"Foundation University Hospital Metropolitano in Atlántico, Colombia."

"Do you know how I got here?"

"*Sí.* Government officials located the wreckage of your plane and brought you here."

"Were there other survivors?"

"*Sí,*" she repeated.

"How many?"

"*Dos.*"

"Can you tell me their condition?"

When she sighed, I wondered if I was going to get a lecture about HIPAA rights.

"There is a gentleman in the room next door. He is in worse condition than you are, but not by much. The other man is not expected to make it."

I was as stunned by her statement as I was by the lack of accent that had been more pronounced in what she'd said to that point.

"Are you American?" I asked.

"I lived there for a while."

I thought about asking where, but did I really care? No. "The guy next door, is his last name Clarkson?"

She rifled through pieces of paper attached to a clipboard. "*Sí.*"

I rested my head on the pillow and closed my eyes, torn between wanting to conjure Sloane's likeness and forcing it away. As if I had a choice.

I opened my eyes when I heard the door again.

"There he is," said Razor Sharp, one of the four founding partners of K19 Security Solutions, the private security and intelligence firm I contracted with but hoped to work for full-time. "How are you feeling?" he asked.

"Better than I expected, given I didn't think I'd be alive."

He smiled and shook my hand, holding on longer than necessary, but I didn't mind. In fact, I welcomed any kind of human contact.

"How's Halo?" Knox Clarkson, the man in the room next door, had been my best friend since his family moved to Newton, Massachusetts, when we were both in high school. I was the one responsible for the nickname that became his code name when, after a backyard game of football, my friend broke his neck and had to wear the so-named contraption for several weeks.

I'd been given my nickname around the same time. It wound up being prophetic when I was named the number one offensive tackle in the country while playing Division I football for the University of Virginia.

"I haven't been in to see him yet, but from what I understand, you'll both be discharged within a few days."

"What about Onyx?"

Razor ran his hand through his spiky ink-black hair. "That news isn't as good."

Should I confess the nurse had just told me our friend and colleague wasn't expected to live?

"As soon as he stabilizes, we'll make arrangements to transport him to a hospital in the States."

"Is that a possibility?"

"He made it through surgery but hasn't come out of the coma he's been in since he was brought here." Razor looked at something on his phone and stood. "I'll be back a little later."

If whatever he read was something about Onyx, I didn't want to know. My mother would say I was a classic Libra—I dodged confrontation and bad news like a champ. I didn't believe in astrological bullshit, but I would be the first to admit that avoidance was my coping mechanism of choice.

***

"I'm going to tell as many people as I can that I love them," Halo said to me a few days later when we buckled into our seats on the private plane that would take us home.

"Me too."

"Even my extended family. My aunts and uncles will all think I'm nuts, but I don't give a shit."

"Huge wake-up call," I muttered.

"Can I ask you something?"

"Shoot."

"You ever think about settling down, getting married, having kids?"

"I didn't before." I mean, I did, but only when my mother reminded me that as an only child, I was responsible for giving her grandchildren. Those reminders came more often after I'd turned twenty-nine.

"It's different now, right?"

It occurred to me that maybe Halo had a specific reason for asking. "Is there anyone you've been, you know, seeing?"

"Negative. What about you?"

"There's someone." What the fuck? Had my life almost ending in a plane crash given me a death wish? If I told Halo the woman I'd been fantasizing about was his sister, I wouldn't live to walk off this plane.

"There is? Who is she?"

"That isn't important right now. If or when that changes, I'll let you know."

"Seriously?"

"She might not feel the same way I do." That was an honest response, considering Sloane would have no way of knowing she even crossed my mind.

"Is it someone I know?"

Shaking my head felt like less of a lie than saying the words out loud. Why hadn't I just kept my stupid mouth shut? I felt a barrier go up between Halo and me, and it was of my making. We'd known each other long enough that he could easily sense when I wasn't telling the truth. Like he just had.

We were quiet the remainder of the flight; I feigned sleep for most of it.

2

Sloane

I bolted upright, drenched in a cold sweat, and covered my face with my hands. The door to my bedroom flung open, and my mother raced in. She sat on the edge of my bed and gently pulled my hands from my face. "What's wrong? Did you have another nightmare?"

I nodded. "How did you know?"

"I heard you cry out."

"What did I say?"

"Nothing decipherable."

Thank God. I'd been dreaming about Tackle, not my brother, as I was sure my mother assumed.

She stroked my hair. "Go back to sleep, *mija.* We don't have to leave for the airport for a few more hours."

She sat between me and the clock on the nightstand and my phone that sat beside it. "What time is it now?"

"A little after eight."

Given that most days I was up by five, I considered eight sleeping in. However, the last few days had been so emotionally draining, my sleep patterns were completely off.

Seven days ago, the day before Thanksgiving, my brother, Knox, whom everyone called Halo, along with his best friend, Landry, whom everyone called Tackle, had been deployed on an intelligence mission on behalf of the US government.

Both my brother and Tackle were former CIA agents who now contracted for the agency through a private intelligence and security company.

Before they left, I'd had a good idea where they were headed. While the information was classified, as a criminal investigator for the US Department of Homeland Security, my security-clearance level was high enough to know the op they'd been hired to carry out involved apprehending a suspected terrorist with ties to the Islamic State.

I'd been tracking the same man's—Abdul Ghafor—communication with known terrorist cells in the US for months. His last confirmed whereabouts were outside Bagram in Afghanistan, but sources had recently spotted him in Colombia.

Thanksgiving Day, twenty-four hours after I watched my mother say a tearful goodbye to her son, my father, a foreign service specialist for the State Department, received a call, informing him that the plane Knox,

Tackle, and two other private intelligence agents were traveling on had disappeared from the radar.

A few hours later, he received word that the plane's wreckage was believed to have been located in Columbia's Macuira National Park, and the DEA agents who found it, reported there were survivors.

An agonizing twelve hours after that, we were told that my brother had been airlifted to a university hospital in Magdalena. His injuries were not believed to be life-threatening.

"What about Tackle?" I asked when my father's call ended. He shook his head and walked over to where Nils and Alice—Tackle's parents—sat with my mother. I held my breath, waiting for him to speak.

"They're reporting two survivors other than Knox."

"Meaning one fatality," said Nils.

Alice gasped and covered her mouth to stifle her keening sobs. My eyes met my mother's; both of us were in tears.

I wrapped my arms around my stomach and rushed out the back door of our house, not knowing where I was going, only that I had to get far enough away that no one would bear witness to my reaction to the news that Tackle—my beloved Tackle—may or may not be alive.

By the time I returned to the house, my father had received an update that, like Knox's, Tackle's injuries were not believed to be life-threatening. Also like Knox, he'd been airlifted to the hospital.

I could no more show my relief than I'd been able to reveal my devastation. No one—not a single living soul—knew my true feelings for my older brother's best friend. Not even the man himself—even though I'd secretly loved him for years.

I was eleven and he was fourteen the day his parents dragged him over to our house a few days after we'd moved in.

Mrs. Sorenson was the head of the neighborhood welcoming committee, and given my brother and her son were the same age, Tackle had been recruited to "show my brother around."

"It's too bad they don't have a daughter your age," my mother had said that day. I was glad they didn't. Given I couldn't take my eyes off Landry, I likely would've ignored her and been scolded for it.

I lay in bed, staring at the ceiling of the room that had been mine for most of my life. It hadn't changed much in the last fifteen years, other than the size of the bed. Four years ago, the twin had been upgraded to a queen when my mother announced she wanted to turn it into a guest room once I moved out. Since I still lived at home and commuted to my job in Boston, my room had remained mine.

It wasn't that I couldn't get a place of my own; I could afford to, even with the sky-high prices of rentals in Boston. But if I did, the few times I had the opportunity to see Tackle would become nonexistent.

I glanced at the clock when the smells of my mother's traditional Venezuelan breakfast wafted up the stairs and into my room. She didn't make *perico* and *arepas* very often. Usually only for special occasions or when she believed one or all of us needed comfort food.

Today I welcomed the eggs scrambled with onions, tomatoes, and butter that she'd season with coriander and annatto powder. My mother would heap the *perico* on top of the *arepas*, which were round cornmeal cakes that looked similar to English muffins but tasted nothing like them.

It was my brother's favorite breakfast. I wondered if she made it in honor of his homecoming, even though he wouldn't be with us until later tonight to eat it.

"The Sorensons will be flying to Washington with us," my mother said as I washed the breakfast dishes and she put them away.

"Was there any doubt they would?"

She shrugged. I knew she found the Sorensons cold at times, but then they probably found her over-the-top emotional. Just because they weren't as effusive as she was didn't mean they weren't as excited to see their son as we were to see Knox. Or that I was.

I took my time getting ready, wanting to strike a balance between looking my best and not overdoing it. After settling on a pair of jeans, black sweater, and military-style boots, I braided my long blonde hair and put on a minimal amount of makeup, knowing that the minute I saw my brother and his best friend, I'd dissolve into tears.

"Are you okay?" my mother asked as we got in the car to drive to the airport.

"I'm fine. Why?"

"You seem nervous."

I shrugged. "I'm anxious."

By the time we arrived at the terminal in Washington, DC, my *anxiety* had increased to the point I was literally shaking.

"*Mija*, I'm worried about you," my mother said, attempting to hold my hand.

"We all handle stress in our own way. Maybe the reality of almost losing my only brother is just now hitting me."

"But he's fine, *mija*."

"I'll feel better when I see him with my own eyes."

"That's them," said my dad, pointing to a plane taxiing in our direction. When I glanced over at Tackle's parents, my eyes met Alice's. She smiled, almost as if she knew I was looking forward to seeing her son as much as my brother.

A crew was waiting to roll a stairway over to the plane after it came to a stop. When the cabin door opened, a man I recognized but wasn't my brother or Tackle, was the first person to step off. His name was Razor Sharp, and he was one of the owners of the company Knox worked for. When he was almost to the bottom stair, an ambulance drove up and parked. Razor walked over to it at the same time I saw my brother come out the door.

"There he is!" squealed my mother. "*¡Gracias a Dios!*"

As I'd anticipated, my eyes filled with tears. He looked a little worse for wear, but not like he'd lived through a plane crash. I gasped when, moments later, Tackle joined him.

He was as battered and bruised as Knox, but he was as beautiful as I'd ever seen him.

He'd grown from a boy to a man in the fifteen years I'd known him. His shoulders were broader, his neck thicker, his arms and legs visibly sculpted even under his clothes and at a distance. One of my favorite things about him was how quickly and easily he smiled—like he was now. Even if he weren't wearing sunglasses, I wouldn't be able to tell who in our huddled group had caught his eye, but in my fantasies, his gaze belonged solely to me.

They'd told us not to, but my mother raced forward to hug my brother anyway. I looked up at my father. As always, the look on his face as he watched her conveyed his love. Like me, his eyes filled with tears as we watched her embrace my brother.

She motioned for us to come closer, and we did. My father hugged Knox while Tackle's father did the same to his son. Over his dad's shoulder, my eyes met the man's I'd loved for as long as I could remember.

I could conjure endless silly fantasies about what his expression meant. Had coming so close to death made him realize he loved me as much as I loved him? Was he as impatient as I to finally feel my body next to his when we got our chance to embrace?

My father's arm brushed mine when he let go of my brother.

"Come here, you," Knox said, pulling me against him. "I love you, Sloane. You know that, right?"

"I love you too, Knox."

"I'm sorry I haven't been a better brother to you."

I squeezed him. "You've always been the best brother a girl could have."

He pulled back and looked into my eyes. "I want us to spend more time together."

"I'd like that."

Out of the corner of my eye, I saw my mother approach Tackle and, behind me, Alice waiting to embrace Knox.

I took a step back, unsure what I should do next. Should I hang around? Go inside and wait?

After my dad hugged Tackle and slapped his back, both men turned to me. "Go ahead, Sloane," said Nils, who I hadn't seen standing beside me. "He's practically your brother too."

I took a couple of steps forward and walked into the open arms of a man I'd never once viewed that way.

"Sloane," he whispered, pulling me close and hugging me harder than Knox had. Every nerve ending, every hair, every cell of my body tingled as I sunk into his embrace. "We need to talk."

When I pulled back to ask what about, I saw Knox watching us.

"Later," Tackle added as I nodded, let go, and stepped away.

"I want you to come home for a while," my mother said, putting her arm through Knox's as we walked into the terminal.

"I will, soon, I promise."

"What do you mean?"

My brother put his hands on our mother's shoulders. "Right now, Onyx needs us." He motioned with his head to where a gurney was being rolled over to the waiting ambulance.

Instead of arguing with him like I, and probably he, expected her to, my mother nodded and looked over at Tackle's parents.

"Will you be staying on too?" I heard Alice ask her son.

When Tackle looked first at my brother, then at me, and back at his mother, I felt my cheeks flush. "I'm coming home for a few days," he murmured.

"You are?" Knox asked.

Tackle nodded. "For a few days," he repeated.

3

Tackle

If we were alone, I'd tell Halo to fuck off. I might even ask him why spending time with a guy in a coma was more important than being with his family. But we weren't alone, and if I hurled all the anger I was feeling at the man who'd been my best friend for more than half of my life, especially in front of our families, it would lead to questions I couldn't answer.

Every single person—my mother, my father, her parents, her brother, hell, even the other people milling about in the terminal—who kept me away from Sloane made me angry. All I could think about was grabbing her hand and getting the fuck out of here.

I couldn't explain the unrelenting need I felt from the minute I looked out the door of the plane and saw her waiting with my family and hers. All I knew was that I couldn't deny I craved her in the same way I'd craved a single drink of water a year ago when I was taken hostage by a band of pirates in the Somali desert. Like then, I needed it—her—to go on living.

I'd told Halo there was a woman, who I wasn't sure felt the same way I did. I hadn't lied. Would Sloane think I'd lost my mind when we were finally alone and I pushed her up against the nearest wall and kissed her like my life depended on it?

I couldn't think about that. If I did, I might not go through with what I had planned, and I *had* to.

"I'd ask if you're okay, but I know you're not," my father said, resting his hand on my shoulder.

"You're right."

"Is there anything your mother and I can do?"

"Give me space." It was the same thing I'd told my parents after I was rescued in Somalia and returned home. The thing I needed then, like now, was space, time alone, room to breathe. No. That wasn't right. I didn't need time alone; I needed time with Sloane. Just the two of us.

My eyes met her questioning ones. The last time I had touched her in a non-brotherly way was the night of her senior prom. She'd looked so damn pretty when I showed up after I drove to her house like my car was on fire, so I wouldn't be late.

That day, Halo had walked into the living room of the apartment he and I shared, looking perplexed.

"What's up?" I'd asked.

"I just got off the phone with my mom. Sloane's date for the prom has the flu."

"That sucks."

"It's her senior prom, man. My mom wants me to fly home and take her, but I've gotta work. Plus, Sloane would never agree to it. I don't know what would be worse. Not going or going with your brother."

"I'll do it," I'd said without thinking.

"You will?"

I told Halo I'd planned to visit my parents that weekend anyway. It wouldn't be a big deal to spend a few hours at a dance.

He hadn't believed my lie about visiting my parents any more than I thought he would, but his only response was to pat me on the back and thank me.

***

After we all said goodbye to Knox—my best friend, her older brother—we caught the next flight back to Boston. The six of us were on our way to the parking structure after the quick flight when I pulled out my phone and typed a text. *Meet me later?*

Sloane's eyes met mine. *Where?*

Where? That was a good question. How would she respond if I asked her to meet me at the Old Orchard Inn? Would she think I'd lost my mind? I sure as hell felt like I had. Instead, I sent her the name of the diner we'd all hung out at as kids.

What time? she messaged back.

An hour? If I had too much time to think about this, I'd probably convince myself that being alone with my best friend's kid sister was the stupidest thing I'd ever done.

I'll be there in forty-five minutes.

"Hey, Dad?" I heard Sloane say when we walked up to our parents' cars, which were parked next to each other. "I need to go into the office for a few hours. Would you mind catching a ride with the Sorensons so Tackle can drop me off there?"

"We can drop you," her father answered.

"There are some things I need to take care of in the city before I head home anyway," I offered.

"I have a better idea," said my father. "You take our car, and we'll catch a ride with Ben and Carolina." He tossed me the keys.

I had no idea if my father had an inkling of what was really going on. He didn't let on like he did. My mother's look, though, made me pray she kept quiet.

"I'll be home later," I said, walking over to hug her.

"If anything changes, let us know, so we don't worry," she whispered.

When Sloane walked to the passenger side of my parents' car, I followed and opened it for her.

She didn't say anything, and neither did I, but the air was thick between us. Was she thinking the same things I was? Did she want me the way I wanted her? Or did she think we were just going to "talk" like I'd said earlier?

"Where to?" I asked after our parents left and I was about to back the car up. "Still want to go to the diner?"

Sloane shook her head. "Boylston and Park."

"What's there?"

"A friend's apartment. She's in Florida with her parents for the rest of the month."

"Sloane—"

"Don't talk, Tackle. Just drive."

I was all for not talking, but I wasn't ready to drive yet. I turned in my seat, reached over, and grabbed the back of her neck. I was close enough to kiss her, but I didn't. I looked into her blue eyes and brushed her honey-blonde hair from her face with my free hand.

"Kiss me," she demanded. "Before you talk yourself out of it."

I brought my lips to hers, and for the second time in my life, I kissed her. The only other time I had was on the night I walked her to her door after her senior prom. I'd planned to kiss her cheek, but at the last second, Sloane had turned her head and kissed my mouth instead.

I held her still as I pushed my tongue between her parted lips, savoring the realness of how she felt after all the hours I'd spent fantasizing about our mouths being fused together. If I were dreaming, I would've put my hand under her sweater, reached inside the cups of her bra, and felt the breasts that had teased me every time I showed up at the Clarksons' backyard pool and she came outside in her barely there bright-orange bikini.

Unable to resist, I acted out my fantasy, shuddering when I felt her pebbled nipple against my palm. I moved her clothes out of my way and took my first taste of what I'd always considered forbidden fruit.

Sloane wove her fingers in my hair and pulled. I took one more lick and looked up at her. "You urging me on or want me to stop?"

"Both," she groaned. "But I don't want whatever is going to happen between us to be in a car in a parking garage."

"Me either." I covered her perfect breast with her bra and pulled her sweater down to her waist. I was so tempted to cup her mound to feel how wet she was for me, but I resisted. I took a deep breath, put the car in gear, and backed out of the parking space.

Sloane didn't look at me once during our drive from the airport to her friend's apartment.

"Should I look for a place on the street?" I asked.

"Her building has parking."

"What is she? A millionaire?" Parking places in Boston went for more than some people paid for a house. To have an apartment in a building where parking was included was like winning the damn lottery.

She turned to me and smiled, which was exactly what I'd been hoping for. "Her father owns the building, so, yeah, I guess you could say she's worth a lot of money."

"No roommates?"

"No roommates, and she won't be back for a couple more weeks. I'm kind of house-sitting."

I couldn't think about that. The idea that I might be able to keep Sloane in bed for days on end was far too appealing.

She pointed to a driveway and pulled a remote out of her bag. The gate opened. "It's that spot," she said, motioning to the one closest to the elevator.

I parked, got out, and walked around the back of the car to open her door. I held my hand out to her, and she took it. "Sloane—"

She put her arms around my waist, grabbed the cheeks of my ass, and pulled me against her. "No more talking, Tackle. Unless it's to tell me how hard you're going to fuck me."

I nearly came in my pants.

4

Sloane

I didn't want to talk. Talking led to conversations. And questions—too many of which I didn't want to answer. They would come, of course. The questions. I might talk big, but it didn't change the fact that I was a twenty-six-year-old virgin.

I knew Tackle well enough that I doubted he'd ask me why outright. At least not at the moment.

My hand shook as I reached out to press the call button for the elevator. When it happened again once we were inside, Tackle reached out too.

"What floor?" he asked.

"Three."

He pushed the number, turned my body to face his, and wrapped one arm around me. "Sloane, am I making you uncomfortable?"

"No."

He put his fingertips on my chin and kissed me. The elevator fantasies I had, didn't have time to play out during our quick three-floor ride. "It's this way." I pointed and led him down the hallway.

"Give me the key," he said when I stopped in front of the door.

My friend kept the blinds closed in the apartment, so it was dark when we walked over the threshold. I would've preferred to keep it that way, but Tackle found a light switch and turned it on.

Before he could ask again if I was uncomfortable, I launched at him. When I practically knocked him over, I realized I may have been too eager. "Oh my God, did I hurt you?"

He laughed, steadied himself, lifted me in his arms, and carried me down the hallway, kissing me breathless as we went.

He eased us both onto the bed and immediately brought his mouth back to mine as we tore at each other's clothes.

He pulled away. "Sloane?"

I closed my eyes, silently begging, pleading, praying that he wasn't about to tell me this was a bad idea or that he'd changed his mind. "What?"

"I don't have any condoms."

"It's okay," I said, trying to get out from under him.

"It isn't okay. We can't—"

"I do." That wasn't exactly true. My friend did. How did I know? I'd been looking for a Q-tip in the bathroom and was stunned to find an unopened box of size extra-large in the cabinet under the sink. I rolled off the bed.

"Wait."

I couldn't face him. "Tackle, please."

"Please what?"

"Don't."

"Turn around."

"Don't," I repeated.

"Please."

I gripped the doorjamb and turned on my heel. I stood before him; the bottom half of my body was still clothed, and the top half was covered in only my bra. I crossed my arm over it.

His eyes met mine. "I just want to look at you. Drop your arm." His eyes trailed down my face to my pink lace bra. "Take it off."

I reached behind me and flicked the clasp. When it came loose, the straps slid down my arms. In the same way I'd launched myself at him, Tackle jumped off the bed, stalked over to me, and covered my bare flesh with the palms of his hands.

"You know how many times…Those damn bikinis."

I might've laughed, but when he sucked my nipple into his mouth, all I could do was groan and grip his bare shoulders.

He covered my other breast with one hand while he unfastened my jeans with the other. "I need these off." He knelt and pulled my jeans and panties down to my knees. "Getting a little ahead of myself," he muttered as he untied my boots. "Hold on to me."

I put my hands back on his shoulders as he took off one boot, then the other.

"Step out."

When I did, he stood. I was completely naked, whereas he still had his pants on. I studied the cuts and bruises on his body.

"It looks worse than it is," he said, perhaps feeling as uncomfortable with his partial nudity as I was with mine. "Where are the condoms?"

"I can get them." Before I could walk away, Tackle grabbed my wrist. "Tell me where they are and wait for me on the bed."

"Under the sink in the bathroom."

He traipsed away while I pulled back the sheets and climbed under them.

When he came back in and set the box on the night table, he smiled. "You're always hiding from me."

"You're the one who's still wearing clothes."

"Always teasing me too."

Tackle dropped his pants, and like an idiot, I gasped.

5

Tackle

There wasn't any question that me being naked in front of Sloane was uncomfortable—for both of us. It also didn't come as a surprise that she wasn't exactly the *femme fatale* she'd played herself off as when we got out of the car earlier. It was as though with every step she took, she turned into the shy eighteen-year-old I took to her senior prom.

That night, I knew she was innocent. It was obvious by the way she'd reacted to me holding her close when we danced. I could still recall the way her pupils had dilated and her breathing became labored the instant her body was flush with mine. She'd even apologized that her hands were sweaty.

But now, eight years later, she had to have had more...experience, right?

"Sloane—"

She bolted upright, reached for her sweater, and held it in front of her. "If you changed your mind, just say so."

"Hey, now," I said, gently pulling her back to lie down. I took the sweater from her hands and tossed it on the floor. There was no way I was going to change my mind, and I prayed she didn't either. I'd come too close to dying, not just once, but many times. The plane crash had been the worst, though. I couldn't imagine leaving this planet not knowing how it felt to hold Sloane's naked body in my arms.

I leaned forward and kissed her. "I want this," I murmured.

"I want it too."

I smiled. "Good."

She rolled to her side, took one of my hands, and put it back on her breast.

"You like that, huh?"

Sloane nodded.

"Me too."

It wasn't easy to take my time. I wanted to grab a condom, roll it on, spread her legs, and finally know how it felt to be inside her. But where Sloane had seemed in a hurry earlier, now she was taking her time, exploring me with her eyes and hands. As painfully hard as I was, I still had to let her.

"Your body…"

"What about it?" I asked.

"It's changed."

I leaned forward and swirled her nipple with my tongue. "So has yours."

She ran her hands from my shoulders down the front of me, stopping when she got to my pecs. "Do you like this too?" she asked, running her finger around my nipple. She laughed when I grabbed her hand. "I guess not."

"Too sensitive right now for that."

I might be able to wait to sink my cock into her heat, but I needed to touch her. I trailed my hand down and pushed open her thighs.

"Oh my God," she groaned when I circled her drenched opening with my fingertip and then pressed against her clit with the pad of my thumb. She grabbed my wrist like I had her hand.

"What's wrong?" I asked, not allowing her to move my hand away. "You need more, Sloane?" I put one finger inside her and then added a second. I couldn't help but breathe a metaphorical sigh of relief that, while she was tight, I didn't feel any kind of barrier. Not that I would know exactly what it felt like since, to my knowledge, I'd never had sex with a virgin.

"Can I touch you?" she whispered.

"Of course you can," I said, guiding her hand to my steel-hard cock. That worried feeling crept back when it seemed like she hadn't touched one before. "Put your hand around me." When she did, I put mine on top of hers. "Harder," I said, squeezing her fingers. "That's it." Damn, it had been too long since I'd been with a woman, and her touch felt so fucking good. "Stop," I groaned.

"Did I do something wrong?"

"No. Not at all." I reached over, grabbed a condom packet, opened it, and rolled it on.

"Good thing they're extra large," Sloane teased when I gritted my teeth.

"I can't wait," I said. I placed my cock at her entrance and eased in. Her fingernails dug into my shoulders, and her eyes opened wide. "We'll take it slow," I said as much to myself as to her. I felt her body softening and slid inside a little farther. "You doing okay, Sloane?" I asked.

"You're so big."

"Why, thank you," I said, sliding in another inch.

Sloane closed her eyes and arched her neck. "More," she moaned.

"You're so wet," I said, allowing myself to thrust deeper.

She opened one eye. "Um, thanks?"

I pulled almost all the way out and then thrust back in, picking up the pace of my movement. When I reached down with one hand and fingered her clit, she almost came off the bed.

I stopped thinking and let my body take over, focusing only on how fucking good Sloane felt. When she met my thrusts, I let myself go, deepening, quickening.

Sloane wrapped her legs around my waist and cried out her release. Seconds later, I followed.

I slowed, but was in no hurry to separate my body from hers. Still inside her, I shifted our two bodies so I didn't crush her slight frame with my weight.

When I felt Sloane trying to wriggle away, I held her still. "Not yet," I said. "Let me feel you."

She remained where she was for a few more seconds. "I need to get up."

"Okay." I pulled out but kept my hand on her waist. "Look at me," I said when she tried to hide her face. She shook her head and tried again to get up, but I wouldn't relent. "Sloane, look at me."

"No."

I put my hand on the side of her face and turned her toward me. "Why are you crying? Did I hurt you?"

"No. Just let me go."

This time, I did and watched her rush off in the direction of the bathroom. I sat up and looked down to remove the condom. "Fuck," I muttered, noticing two things. First, it was ripped. Second, I could see faint traces of blood. I heard the shower go on and made my way down the hallway. The door was closed, and when I tried the handle, I found it was locked.

"Hey, Sloane? You okay in there?"

"I'm fine," I heard her holler back.

"Why'd you lock the door?"

"I don't know. Habit. I'll be out in a sec." I heard the water shut off a literal second later. The door opened, and Sloane scooted past me with a towel wrapped around her.

I went in, disposed of the condom, and got in the shower to rinse off. After getting out, I grabbed a towel, put it around my waist, and padded back to the bedroom.

"Hey, where'd you go?" I shouted as I walked out to the main room. I didn't get any response, and the place wasn't big enough that she wouldn't have heard me.

I went back into the bedroom to look for my clothes. As I pulled on my pants, I heard an alert on my phone. I swiped the screen and looked at Sloane's text.

Got called into work. Lock the door behind you.

What...the...fuck? When I tried to call her to say those exact words, it went straight to voicemail.

***

Three days later, I still hadn't been able to reach her. I tried calling; every time, it went to voicemail. I stopped by her parents' house, but other than to say hello, I couldn't think of any way to find out when Sloane was last home, so I asked how she was. That alone got me an odd look from both of them. I even went back into the city and staked out the damn apartment building.

Finally, I decided to say fuck it and called Halo.

"How's Onyx?" I asked when he answered.

"No change."

"Thought I'd head down to DC."

"I can keep you updated if you don't feel like it."

"Nah. I'm getting bored up here anyway."

"Let me tell ya, brother. It ain't exactly fun times around here."

"I stopped in to see your parents yesterday."

"Yeah, my mom try to feed you?"

I laughed. "I told her straight off I couldn't stay."

"It was nice of you to stop by. I feel kinda bad for not going home like you did."

"Have you talked to them?"

"No, and I should. I'll call when we hang up. You really headed this way?"

"Yep. I'll swing by the apartment and drop my stuff, then I'll head over."

I drove by Halo's parents' house one more time on my way out of town, but not for any good reason. Unless I happened to catch her going in or out, I wouldn't know if Sloane was there anyway.

At first, I was worried when I couldn't reach her. Then I got pissed. I was almost to the point where I didn't care.

I mean, how awkward would it have been if, after having a good, solid fuck, Sloane thought it meant we were a couple? I should be grateful she'd bailed before I had to.

Two things didn't sit right with me, though. Actually, it was more than that, but two main things. First, the broken condom. Second, the blood. Had I been right when I initially thought Sloane seemed inexperienced? Or worse, had I hurt her? If I had, why the fuck hadn't she said so? Was that why she'd been crying?

It occurred to me that I probably should've told her about the condom right away, but shit, what chance had I had? I hadn't expected her to disappear while I was in the shower. Nor did I expect her to ghost me.

When I got to Logan, I parked in the private lot where K19 Security Solutions kept several spots. As I rode from there to the terminal in one of the shuttles, I decided to try one more time.

I pressed the button, not even bothering to hold the phone up to my ear. Like every other time I called, it didn't even ring. It occurred to me that maybe she'd blocked my number.

If so, she wouldn't get the text I sent anyway. Might as well keep that simple too.

Condom broke.

***

Apart from the briefings we had to give about what went down on our flight to Columbia, Halo was right. Being in DC was a drag. We went to see Onyx every day. Better put, we went to see Monk, who was there all day and night from what we could tell.

I felt for the guy. I mean, he'd been the handler on the op that went sideways, but there wasn't a damn thing he could've done differently.

No one, least of all Onyx, would've believed Corazón, the woman who'd almost killed us all and who Onyx had been sleeping with, was a double agent.

Damn women. Who would've thought Sloane would ever pull the shit she was, either. I shook my head. That wasn't fair. Just because my best friend's sister had decided she didn't want anything more to do with me didn't put her on par with a fucking traitor and murderer.

"Ready?" Halo asked, coming out of the bathroom.

"Yep." We were on our way to the hospital one last time before we caught a flight back to Boston to spend the holidays with our families, who always got together at least two or three times between Christmas and New Year's Day. Part of me considered not going home, but that wouldn't have been fair to my parents. I'd figure out a way to politely decline to go along with whatever they did with Halo's parents. Either that, or I'd show up just to see how Sloane would react.

"I'm sure you've already briefed Doc about this, but what went down that day?" Monk asked when we were getting ready to leave to catch our flight home.

I rubbed the back of my neck, wishing he hadn't asked, especially today. "It was a major Charlie Foxtrot, Monk."

Halo nodded. "I don't know what went on in the cockpit, but when we were just past Aruba, all hell broke loose. It all happened so fast. We heard a shot being fired and stormed the front of the plane. Onyx had taken a direct hit, and Corazón had her gun turned our way when I fired."

"By that time, the plane was already taking a dive. I didn't think there was any way we'd live through it," I added.

I tuned Halo out when I heard him telling Monk how almost dying had changed his outlook on life. I'd heard it too many times. When he nudged me, I gave Monk the same song and dance, telling him how every time I wanted to put something off until the next day, I thought better about it. But was that even true? If I had really wanted to find Sloane, I could've. I could've grown the balls to call her house and try to talk to her. Or ask her parents when she was expected home. But I hadn't. I'd allowed myself to sink back into my comfort zone of avoiding confrontation. So was I really living every day like it was my last? Fuck no.

"You all right?" Halo asked when we left the hospital.

"Yeah. I'd rather not have to talk about that day ever again."

"I hear ya."

We'd just stepped off the elevator in the parking garage when Halo got a call.

"Tackle and I are about to head to the airfield," I heard him say to whoever was on the other end. A few seconds later, he hung up.

"What was that about?" I asked.

"That was Striker. I've decided not to accept K19's offer."

"Why not?"

"You can drive," he said once we were in the car.

"Why not?" I repeated without turning on the engine.

"I gave it a lot of thought, and I'm just not ready to make that kind of commitment."

"What are you going to do?"

"I don't know yet, but maybe some PI work."

Striker had called me a few days ago. I told Halo to say the same thing I had. "Tell him you need more time."

"Have you given them an answer?"

"No."

"What about you? What are you going to do?"

"I'm thinking about working for my dad."

My dad owned a construction company and had made it clear that if I wasn't ready to go back into intelligence either now or in the future, he had a job waiting for me.

"Is that what you did, told them you needed more time?"

I nodded.

"Nothing like surviving a plane crash to make a guy reassess his life," Halo mumbled.

"Listen, I'm sorry I've been so distant." It wasn't his fault his sister had had sex with me once and then decided she didn't want anything to do with me.

"We okay?" Halo asked.

"Always." When we walked into the terminal, Striker was waiting. I shook his hand and told them I'd be at the bar.

"How'd it go?" I asked when Halo came and joined me a little while later.

"He gave me a side job."

"Doing what?"

"Missing person. Apparently, Tara Emsworth disappeared shortly after Thanksgiving."

"Name sounds familiar."

"She's one of Razor's wife's best friends."

"That's right. Mercer's wife's too." Both men were guys we worked for at K19 Security Solutions.

"So your job is to find her?"

Halo nodded. "Wanna help? And by that, I mean come up with a plan."

"Sure, I can do that." No way in hell I'd take a mission, though. Maybe never again.

When I drove up to Halo's parents' house a couple of hours later, he invited me in. Instead, I told him I'd come by that night. It was obvious it bugged him. No other time that I could remember had I refused to at least say hello. However, my reason for not wanting to now, was something I couldn't admit or explain.

6

Sloane

I saw the car pull up and hoped Tackle would park and come in. I equally hoped Knox would get out and Tackle would drive away. My second wish came true.

Tomorrow was Christmas, and if my parents didn't invite his over, they would the following day. I thought about telling them I had a work emergency requiring I travel out of town, but why would I lie to my parents, ruin Christmas for them, just to avoid my brother's best friend, a man who now had a different and more significant descriptor—the one who took my virginity?

When I was growing up, we had plenty of ruined holidays when my father's work with the State Department took him away from our family. He'd been gone more than he was home, at least until we moved to Newton, outside of Boston. I hadn't asked and never would, but I assumed my mother had given him an ultimatum of some kind, and that was the only reason he'd agreed to the move. Even though his travel was cut to twenty-five percent of what it had been, it was still hard on her when he left for weeks at a time. Sometimes, at night, I'd hear her crying after we'd both gone to bed.

The day my brother announced he was going to work for the CIA, my parents had a terrible argument. It got so bad, I left the house. But not before I heard her demand my father forbid Knox from taking the job.

She didn't get her way, and for the six months after their fight, she'd let my father know loud and clear how unhappy my brother's decision made her. It was the only time in my life I thought they might get a divorce. In the end, they'd made up, in part because my brother seemed happy.

Then when Knox was kidnapped in Somalia, my mother went into a downward spiral. Fortunately, my brother was rescued within days, but that didn't change the fact that my father had paid dearly by way of burnt meals, the silent treatment, and who knew what behind closed doors.

Next was the plane crash. Her emotional state was so fragile during those endless hours when we waited to hear who the survivors were that she'd leaned on my dad. When we found out Knox was injured but alive, I think she was so thankful, she forgot to be angry with either of them.

That Knox had promised he wouldn't take on any missions until after the new year, and maybe not even then, had elevated her mood, made obvious by the extent to which our house had turned into a Christmas wonderland.

Perhaps this time around, she punished my father through his wallet, given the amount of holiday decorations seemed to quadruple.

"Sloane?" I heard my mother call from downstairs. "Your brother is home!"

"I'll be right there," I hollered back. Before going downstairs, I powered on my phone, thought about unblocking Tackle's number, but shut it down again without doing so.

I knew I was behaving childishly by avoiding him, but after rushing from the apartment that fateful day, I'd set something in motion I had no idea how to stop. I asked myself why I'd felt compelled to throw on my clothes and race away, but I never came up with a good answer.

Mainly, I guess it was because I couldn't face him after he'd witnessed my tears. I'd escaped to the bathroom without answering when he asked why I was crying. I didn't expect that he'd drop it, and there was no way I could explain it to him.

Because after all these years, I finally had sex with the one man I'd waited for. And it was as amazing and wonderful as I'd hoped it would be. I'd had my first orgasm under a hand that wasn't my own, and it was so mind-blowingly spectacular that I'd *cried.*

"Hey, peanut, whatcha doin' up here?" asked Knox, coming into my room.

I walked over and hugged him. "Avoiding the elf-fest downstairs as much as possible."

He laughed and messed my hair like he'd do when we were kids. "Everything okay with you?"

"Of course. Why?" *Jesus.* Had Tackle said something to him?

"You look like you haven't been sleeping."

I turned, studied my face in the mirror, and pinched the bags under my eyes. "You know how it gets right before Christmas, with the extreme right-wing evangelicals fighting with the American Association for the Advancement of Atheism."

He sat down on the bed. "Really?"

I shook my head. "No, but with the increase in large groups of people gathering in one place...You get it."

"Yeah. I guess."

I sat beside him. "How's Onyx?"

"No change."

"Shit. I'm sorry."

"To be honest, I'm more worried about Tackle."

Oh, no. "Why?"

"He's not himself."

"In what way?" I asked, trying to keep my voice from sounding frantic.

"I don't know, exactly. He's been distant."

"You both went through something unimaginable."

"True. It seems like more. I probably shouldn't say anything, but on the plane ride from Columbia home, he mentioned there was someone in his life. A woman he wasn't sure felt the same way about him as he felt for her."

"Oh. Wow," I said, even though inside I was screaming. *What in the ever-loving fuck?* There was a woman in his life, and yet, he'd had sex with me? On his way back from the airport, no less. Worked in a booty call with me so he didn't jump the bones of the woman who wasn't a sure thing. The *asshole.* There was my answer. That's why I ran. Somewhere deep inside, I knew I didn't mean anything to him. It wasn't just that I didn't mean as much to him as he meant to me; it was that I didn't mean jack shit. God, I was as much of an idiot as he was pond scum.

My brother was still talking, but I'd stopped listening. "Sloane?"

"What?"

"You haven't seen him around town with anyone, have you?"

"Sorry, I don't keep tabs on your friends, Knox."

He cocked his head.

"Sorry," I repeated. "No, I haven't seen him at all, let alone with someone."

"Right." He stood. "I just can't believe the guy who's been my best friend all these years didn't tell me he was dating someone."

"I don't know what to say."

He nodded. "We should probably get down there before Mom comes looking for us."

"It's you she won't let out of her sight. I'm part of the woodwork."

Knox rolled his eyes and messed my hair again. "The peanut gallery feeling sorry for herself?"

"Actually, I wouldn't mind disappearing for a while."

Knox's eyes hooded. "Don't joke about that, Sloane."

I sighed. "I'm sorry. I didn't mean anything by it."

"That reminds me, there's a job I'm taking on after the holidays."

"You are? Have you lost your mind? Do not tell Mom, especially today."

"It's not a mission. Not really. Missing person."

"Oh."

"She's a friend of the wives of a couple of the guys I work with."

"I hope she turns up."

He walked over to the window and looked outside. "Me too." He turned back to me. "He didn't even come inside to say hello," he mumbled as he walked out of my bedroom.

I followed him downstairs and into the kitchen when I heard our mother barking orders at him about what she needed help with.

"Go relax. I can do this," I told him.

"I don't mind. I haven't done much other than sit by a guy's bedside for the last couple of weeks." He looked over his shoulder and then leaned closer to me. "Think we can talk her into opening presents earlier tonight?"

"Why?"

"I'm an old man, sis. Staying up until midnight just to open a couple of presents seems…unnecessary."

"She thought you were dead. You really want to go there?"

He laughed and shook his head. "Yeah. Maybe next year."

"Plus, we won't be done cooking until then."

Every year, my mother insisted we make *all the food*. It was one reason she invited Tackle's family over on Christmas Day. We'd never be able to eat all of it ourselves.

The traditional *pernil*, or whole pork shoulder, had been roasting in the oven since yesterday. Today, we'd be making *hallacas,* which were like tamales but wrapped in plantain leaves instead of corn husks, along with *pan de jamón.* Of all the Venezuelan Christmas foods my mother insisted be made every year, the puff pastry filled with ham, raisins, olives, and bacon was my favorite. This year, though, it didn't sound that good.

In fact, by mid-afternoon, I felt so sick to my stomach that I went upstairs to lie down. When I woke up, it was dark and I had no idea what time it was. I thought about getting up to check, but must've fallen back to sleep because, when I opened my eyes again, it was daylight.

Shit. I'd missed *Niño Jesús'* presents. Why hadn't anyone woken me up?

I sat on the edge of the bed, but when I felt the same nausea as yesterday, I lay back down. Great. Christmas and I was sick. At least I had an excuse not to socialize with the Sorensons and their asshole son.

I still couldn't believe he'd had sex with me when he was involved with another woman. It made me so mad that I clenched my fist and pounded on the mattress.

"*Mija*, is everything okay?" my mom asked, opening my bedroom door. Did she suddenly have supersonic hearing? She sat on the side of the bed and brushed my hair from my forehead. "Are you feeling any better? You don't have a fever."

I moved her hand away, jumped out of bed, and raced toward the bathroom. After emptying the contents of my stomach, I held the wall as I made my way back.

"Sorry, Mom, but you should stay away from me in case this is contagious."

She sighed but, thankfully, left.

When I woke two hours later, I felt a lot better. I thought about staying in bed anyway, but I was starving. I changed my clothes and decided I could shower after I ate, so I put my hair up in a messy bun and went downstairs. At the same time I hit the bottom landing, the front door opened.

"Anyone home?" I heard Tackle's mother, Alice, holler out. If she and I hadn't come face-to-face, I would've turned around and raced back up the stairs.

"Oh, Sloane. It's good to see you. Are you feeling better?"

"A little bit."

She stepped aside, and Nils came in, followed by Tackle.

"Merry Christmas," I said, rushing from the stairs into the kitchen. I grabbed a bowl from the cupboard and loaded it with equal amounts of *pernil* and *pan de jamón*.

One of the things I liked about the house I grew up in was that it had a back staircase, which meant I could get to my bedroom without having to face our company again.

I filled a water bottle and was a few steps up when I heard footsteps.

"Where do you think you're going?" Tackle asked.

"Where does it look like? Leave me alone. I'm sick," I said without looking at him.

"Sloane, we need to talk."

I turned halfway and leaned up against the wall. "Knox filled me in. Don't worry, I won't tell."

He stepped on the bottom stair.

"No farther," I said, holding up my water bottle like a weapon.

"What does that mean 'you won't tell'?"

"Is she here?"

When he took another step up, I took two.

"You saw my mom when she came in."

"Not her. Your girlfriend."

"My girlfriend? What the fuck are you talking about? You're delirious. Let me get that for you." He grabbed the water bottle and my bowl of food and squeezed past me.

"Hey!" I shouted after him, but by then, he was already in my bedroom. "You need to leave," I said, motioning toward the door.

"Nope. Not going anywhere until you agree to talk to me."

"We have nothing to talk about. Not to mention if you stay up here, my brother is going to come looking for you. What reason will you give him for being in my bedroom?"

He stepped onto the threshold. "You're right, but we need to talk."

I shook my head. "We don't."

"Sloane, what happened—"

"First of all, lower your voice. And second, I'm more than happy to pretend like it was all a bad dream if that's what you want."

He rubbed his chest with one hand. "Wow. Was it really that bad? Is that why you took off? I've never had anyone—"

"Just shut up and go away," I said, giving him a hard shove. It was far enough that I could close the door, but he stuck his hand out and stopped it. He came back inside and shut it behind him.

"Look, I'm sorry. Okay? You're right. What we did never should've happened."

"I didn't say that."

"You're willing to pretend it was a bad dream? Sounds like you said exactly that."

When he sighed and looked up at me with those gorgeous green eyes, I wanted to fall into his arms and beg him to forgive me, not just for being a bitch to him now, but for racing out that day and blocking his calls since. But there was still the matter of the "woman in his life."

"Why are you here? There's nothing to talk about. If you're afraid I'm going to tell someone and it'll get back to *her,* don't worry. My lips are sealed."

"I don't know—" Tackle went silent when we heard footsteps coming up the stairs. "Answer your fucking phone when I call you," he half spat, half whispered before opening the door and stepping into the hallway.

"What's going on?" I heard Knox ask.

"I helped Sloane bring some stuff up from downstairs."

"How's she feeling?"

"Not sure." At first, I thought they'd walked away, but Tackle's next words sounded like they came from right outside my door. "Except she's really fucking grouchy."

"Usually is when she's sick. Takes after our mom."

This time, I was sure I heard two sets of feet going downstairs.

7

Tackle

"You hungry?"

I was. Halo's mom was a great cook, and every year, I looked forward to coming over here to eat the traditional Venezuelan food she made.

My parents were straight-up American, but both sets of my grandparents had immigrated here from Scandinavia. Outside of Swedish meatballs, which never tasted as good as they sounded, my mom didn't make much food from her parents' homeland.

I followed Halo into the kitchen, ready to heap a plate with food, but found I wasn't as hungry as I thought I was. My conversation with Sloane had been so damn weird.

Under any other circumstances, I would go straight back upstairs and get to the bottom of the weird shit she'd said. *If you're worried it'll get back to her, don't be.* Back to who? That was only one of the things she'd said that made no sense. Like her asking if my girlfriend was with me. Where had that come from? I hadn't had a girlfriend since college, and even then, they hadn't lasted very long.

"What do you think is wrong with her?" I asked.

Halo looked up from the roast pork he was devouring. "Sloane?" He shrugged. "Probably the flu. She's hiding out so she doesn't get everyone else sick."

I leaned forward. "She was saying some crazy shit."

Halo stopped eating. "Like what?"

"She asked if my girlfriend was here."

"Oh."

I sat back in my chair. "That doesn't seem to surprise you."

"Yeah. Sorry, man. That's on me. I kinda asked if she'd seen you around with anyone."

"Why?"

"On the plane, you said there was someone but you weren't sure she felt the same way you did."

"Halo, what the fuck?" I muttered, trying to keep my voice down. "I told you that in confidence."

He leaned forward like I had. "What's with all the mystery, anyway? Since when don't you tell me about a chick you're into?"

"Since I stopped referring to them as chicks and started calling them women."

He pushed back his chair and went to get more food. "I didn't realize it was a damn secret. What is she? A teacher from our high school?"

Worse. Way worse, but I couldn't tell him that. "It doesn't matter anymore. Like I said, she wasn't as into me as I was her."

He sat back down and shoved more food into his mouth. "So who was she?"

"I just told you it doesn't matter."

He shook his head, got up from the table, and put his plate on the counter. Without another word, he stalked off in the direction of the living room.

After making sure he was staying put for a few minutes at least, I went into the hallway and pulled out my phone.

When I couldn't decide what to say to Sloane, I shoved it back in my pocket.

An hour later, I decided there was no point in my sticking around here any longer. Halo was being a dick, answering every question I asked either with a one-word answer or nothing at all. Sloane hadn't shown her face again, not that I'd expected her to.

"Where are you off to?" Halo asked when I grabbed my jacket from the front hall closet.

"Goin' to the grill."

"Mind if I come along?"

"No, but you sure you want to?"

"Look, it pisses me off that you didn't say anything to me about whoever she is, but I get it. Like you said, she isn't into you." Halo grabbed his jacket. "It isn't—?"

"Who?"

He shook his head. "Never mind."

"Who were you going to ask me about?"

"Shit. I can't recall her name. Anyway, I heard she was married."

"How could you know someone is married if you can't remember her name?"

"I can picture her. What the hell was her name?"

I was so relieved he didn't ask me if it was Sloane that he could give me shit all night about women whose names he couldn't remember.

I was about to get into the car when something caught my eye. I looked up and saw Sloane watching us from her bedroom window. I waited until Halo got in before I raised my hand. By then, she was gone.

The place we called the grill's real name was the Biltmore, and it had been around since prohibition days. Back then, it was a speakeasy. Now, it was a dive bar, but with great food. Not that I was hungry.

Halo and I made our way through the crowd until we got to the back, where guys we knew from high school usually hung out.

"Tony, how the hell are you?" I asked, shaking the hand of a guy I'd played football with when he approached to say hello.

"Hey, Tackle. I'm good." He leaned in closer than necessary in the noisy jam-packed bar. "My dad said he heard you and Halo had a close call."

"Don't know what you're talking about, my friend," I said, gripping his shoulder in a way that answered him, yet warned him not to continue talking about it.

"I'm glad you're both okay."

"Appreciate it. Whatcha drinkin'?"

"Same ol' Sammy," he said, holding up a bottle of Sam Adams.

"Hey, Halo?" I pointed at Tony's bottle, and he gave me a thumbs-up.

An hour later, my phone and Halo's both lit up with text messages. "Onyx is awake," I yelled, pumping my fist in the air. I looked at Halo, whose eyes were brimming with tears like mine were.

"It says he's bitching about how Monk never shut up the whole time he was out. What do you think that means?"

"No idea, but if he's talking, we should be celebrating."

"Agreed. Shots for the house on Tackle and me," Halo shouted to the bartender. It would cost us a fortune, given how packed the place was, but who gave a shit. Onyx, our brother-in-arms, was awake.

By the end of the night, I'd had too many beers, listened to too much bullshit, but felt better than I had in months. "We should call a cab," I said to Halo, who was just as lit as I was. "I'll come get my car tomorrow."

"Nah, I called Sloane."

"Say what? You called your sister? She's sick, asshole."

Halo shook his head and took another swig of his beer. "She said she felt better."

"It's snowing, and it's two in the morning. God, you're a jerk."

"What's your problem? Have you forgotten all the other times Sloane picked us up from this very same bar?"

Had she? I guess so. Damn, I was just as much of a jerk as he was. "She know I'm with you?"

Halo looked over at me with scrunched eyes. "Who the fuck else would I be with? I'm beginning to think you got some kind of brain damage when that plane crashed."

"I'm taking a cab." I pulled out my phone to call one when I saw a familiar car drive up.

Sloane didn't look at either her brother or me when we climbed in: him in the front seat, me in the back.

"Tackle said I was an asshole for calling you, sis. Forgive me?"

"If he's as drunk as you are, I'd much rather you call me than try to drive. Then, you would be an asshole."

My eyes met hers in the rearview, and I wished so much that we were alone and I could get her to talk to me. I rested my head against the seat and closed my eyes, remembering in vivid detail—which was surprising in my inebriated state—how every inch of her body looked naked. "God, Sloane," I groaned.

"Tackle!" I heard her yell. "Wake the hell up and get out of the car." I raised my head and saw she was parked in front of my parents' house.

"Sorry 'bout this," I said, reaching over the seat to pat her shoulder. Halo was slouched up against the passenger door, mouth hanging open, and snoring. "And I'm sorry about the condom."

"What did you say?" she asked as I was opening the door to climb out.

"I sure wish you hadn't left that day," I slurred, suddenly realizing I was a lot more drunk than I'd thought.

I looked back over at Halo to make sure he was still asleep, and touched her neck with the tip of my finger.

When she shuddered and leaned her head against my hand, I knew she wished she hadn't, either.

"Take him home and come back."

She moved away from me. "You've lost your mind."

"You know you want me again, Sloane. Just as much as I want you."

She turned and looked at me over the seat. "You're off-your-ass drunk, Tackle."

"So?"

"Get the hell out of my car."

When she turned around to face the front again, I could see the glimmer of a smile. I moved her hair out of my way and put my lips where my fingertip had been.

"Where are we?" groaned Halo, trying to sit up.

"Unblock me," I whispered before getting out of the car and watching her drive away.

8

Sloane

When I woke the next morning feeling just as sick as I had the day before, I cursed both my brother and Tackle for calling me in the middle of the night to give them a ride home. I meant what I said, though. I was glad they had rather than try to drive themselves.

I rolled over and went back to sleep, thankful that I didn't have to get up and go to work for the rest of the week.

"How are you this morning, *mija?*" my mother asked, coming into my bedroom and sitting on the side of my bed. She felt my forehead. "Still no fever. Do you want to try to eat something?"

Nothing I could think of sounded appealing.

"I'll bring you something."

I fluffed my pillow and rested my head on it. Why was I so tired? And why did I have to get sick at Christmas when I was already off work? Actually, no. I didn't have the kind of job where I could afford to take sick leave. Investigations didn't stop because the person responsible fell ill.

"Try eating some toast," my mother said, coming back into my room with a tray that had far more on it than toast. Just the scent of the two roses she put in a small vase was turning my stomach. "Can you take these away?" I asked, handing her the flowers.

My mother raised a brow.

"What?"

"Your symptoms are…interesting."

"Please. Just take them." I shoved the vase in her direction on my way to the bathroom.

"Hey, sorry about last night," said Knox, who met me in the hallway. I held up one finger and raced past him. When I came out, he was leaning against the wall.

"Sorry," I muttered.

"Are you feeling any better at all?"

"I thought so, but now, not so much."

Knox followed me into my room and pulled a chair over when I got back in bed. He leaned forward and rested his elbows on his knees. "I screwed up."

"How?"

"Tackle told me the thing about the woman in confidence. I never should've mentioned it to you."

"What your friends do is none of my concern, Knox."

"He said you asked about his girlfriend."

"I was making a joke." I sounded pissy even to myself. I hoped Knox would attribute it to my being sick rather than wonder why talking about Tackle and his *girlfriend* made me so mad.

I picked up a piece of the dry toast my mother had brought to me. One wouldn't think eating the equivalent of a roof shingle would taste any good, but I was hungry enough that it did. When that stayed down, I tried some of the chunks of fruit she'd also brought.

Why didn't I eat more cantaloupe? I mean, God, was there anything better? And the strawberries? *Wow.* Where had she gotten fruit this good in December?

"Are you okay?"

I opened my eyes, which had been shut in food ecstasy, and studied my brother. "Yeah, why?"

"You look like Tackle and I did after spending a couple of days in the Somalian desert with no food and little water."

"I was sick."

"Right. Anyway, if you could forget I said anything about Tackle's...uh...friend, I'd appreciate it. I guess she isn't as into him as he was her."

I was tempted to pick up the bowl of fruit and hurl it at my brother, but only because he was sitting in front of me and Tackle wasn't. I guess I had my answer as to why he was in such a big hurry to make nice with me. *She* wasn't that into him, so he'd get it where he could.

After Knox left, I rested my head against the pillow and thought about last night. Remembering Tackle's finger on my neck, and then his lips, sent a shudder running through me now like it had then.

"You know you want me again, Sloane. Just as much as I want you," he'd said. Want him again? No. I wanted him forever. He wasn't a slice of pizza I wanted another bite of. I wanted to wake up next to him every morning for the rest of my life.

I'd spent plenty of afternoons, when I was a teenager, writing Sloane Sorenson over and over again on a piece of paper that, afterward, I'd rip to shreds. I even came up with names for the children I fantasized we'd have one day. Not names so much as one name. *Landry.* Whether we had a boy or a girl first, that's what I'd want to name the baby.

God, how long had it been since I thought about any of that? Silly, childish fantasies—that's all they were. The reality was, I'd been a "I just almost died and I need to get laid" booty call.

After eating the rest of the fruit and the toast, I decided I felt good enough to take a shower. When I finished, I felt like I needed a nap, so I took one. When I woke again, I could hear voices from downstairs.

I'd heard one in particular often enough that I recognized it immediately. What the hell was Tackle doing here so early? I rolled over and checked the time. Noon? I'd slept another three hours?

"Hey, you awake?" asked Knox, sticking his head in my room.

"If I wasn't, I would be now."

"Tackle's here. We were hoping we could take you out to thank you for picking us up last night."

"Why? So I can be the designated driver again?"

"I didn't mean it like that. We were thinking lunch or dinner."

The look on my brother's face almost made me cry. I thought back to the day at the airport and how he'd said he wanted to spend more time with me. "I was joking. That sounds really nice. When?"

"Now. Or, um, later. Whatever you want."

"I am hungry."

"Get ready and we'll go. What do you feel like? Or should we just pick something?"

"Pizza."

"You got it."

Knox backed out of the room and went downstairs. I could hear him tell Tackle that I'd agreed to go with them, but I didn't catch his response.

After brushing my teeth, I got dressed, put my hair up in a bun, and sat down to lace up my boots. Was this a good idea? Was Tackle trying to make things seem "normal" between us? Would he treat me like his kid sister the same way Knox did? If so, it would kill me.

I slowly made my way down the stairs, thinking that when I reached the bottom, I'd tell them I wasn't feeling well enough to go with them after all.

However, when my eyes met Tackle's, who was standing by the door, I decided not to.

Like at the airfield, I imagined he was imploring me. To do what this time? Forgive him? Tell him I understood, and while my heart was breaking knowing that he and I would never have the kind of relationship I'd longed for in my fantasies, at least when the time came that I met, fell in love, and married another man, I would do so knowing that at least once in my life, I'd had sex with my first crush—my first love?

"Where's Knox?" I asked.

"Outside, talking to your parents."

"Oh." I opened the front hall closet and pulled out a jacket.

"Here, let me," he said, taking it from my hands and holding it out for me.

"Thanks," I said, peering over my shoulder. He'd leaned in close, and his eyes were closed.

"You smell so good." He inhaled as if I were a flower.

"Um, thanks." I tried to take a step away, but his hands remained on my shoulders.

"I know this isn't ideal, but I'd hoped that, after we eat, I could convince you to meet me somewhere private so we can talk."

When the front door opened, he removed his hands and I took two quick steps forward. "Ready?" I asked when Knox saw me standing there.

"If you are."

When we drove up in front of Max & Millie's, Knox told us to get a table and that he'd park and meet us inside.

"This is your favorite pizza place, right?" Tackle asked, holding the door open for me.

"Can't beat it."

"Yeah, it's my favorite too."

Millie led us to a booth. Rather than sitting across from me, Tackle sat beside me.

"This is a little awkward," I mumbled with a nervous laugh.

Tackle scooted closer, crowding me against the wall. "Not awkward at all. I can touch you all I want, and Halo will never know."

"I think he'll notice. Besides, who says I want you to touch me?"

"You do." He moved farther away from me when we saw Knox headed our way.

The guys ordered a pitcher of beer, but the thought of it turned my stomach. "I'll just have a glass of water with lemon," I told our waitress, who looked like she was just out of high school.

"You were in here a few nights ago, weren't you?" she asked Tackle.

"Uh, maybe. I don't remember."

"Yeah, it was you." She continued staring at him long enough that I thought about asking him to move so I could claw her eyeballs from her head.

"Ahem, if it wouldn't be too much trouble, we'd like to order."

"Sure thing, honeybunch. Go ahead." She still hadn't looked at me.

I reached over and put my hand on Tackle's arm. "Isn't that funny, baby?" I said in the most annoying, over-the-top, drippingly sweet voice I could. "She called me honeybunch, just like you do."

Knox laughed so hard he spit out his drink of beer. Tackle put his hand on mine. "Sorry, miss, but I don't allow anyone to call her honeybunch but me." He brought my hand to his lips and kissed the back of it while Knox kept laughing.

"You're a lucky girl," the waitress muttered. "I'll be back in a minute with your drinks." She walked away, ignoring my request to order food.

I pulled my hand from Tackle's, picked up my menu, and buried my heated cheeks in it.

"That was great," said Knox, nudging me under the table with his foot.

The waitress returned a few minutes later with the guys' beer and water for me. No lemon, of course.

"Chicks," muttered Knox, noticing.

"Chicks? What are you? From the seventies?"

Tackle laughed and shook his head. "That's the same thing I told him the other day."

Both of their heads turned when two women came in.

"That's who I was talking about," said Knox, pointing to one of them who had taken a seat but left her sunglasses on.

Tackle fidgeted and looked back at the menu.

"What the heck is her name?" mumbled Knox. Tackle pretended like he hadn't heard him.

"Who is she?" I asked.

"Just someone we—ouch! *Shit*. Why'd you kick me?" my brother said to the man sitting beside me.

I was just about to ask Tackle to move so I could excuse myself when one of the women stood and walked toward our table.

"Hello, Knox. Hi, Landry," she said. Evidently, my cloaking device had kicked in, rendering me invisible.

"Hi. I'm Sloane," I said, not that she responded. Like the waitress, she couldn't take her eyes off Tackle.

"Hey, Nick," he said.

"I'm sorry to interrupt. Do you have a minute?"

"Now isn't a great—"

"I won't keep you. Just for a minute."

"Excuse me." Tackle slid from the booth and followed her into the bar area.

"Her name is Nick?" I asked.

Knox's gaze followed them. "I remember now; it's actually Claudette."

"Why does he call her Nick?"

"It's her last name. Everyone called her that back in high school. Although, that isn't her name anymore. She's married, but of course I can't remember her husband's name."

"Why were you talking about her?"

"I thought maybe that was the woman Tackle was interested in. Then I remembered she was already hitched."

I grimaced. "Hitched? Who are you?"

"Quit busting my chops."

"Sure thing, King Cliché."

Knox didn't appear to have heard me. His focus was on Tackle and "Nick."

"Oh, shit," he said under his breath.

"What?" I leaned forward at the exact, right moment to see Tackle embrace her. "They have history?" I asked.

"You can't tell him I said anything."

I nodded. "Okay."

"They were on and off in high school. He's always had a soft spot for her." Knox took a drink of his beer. "He's headed back this way."

"Listen," Tackle said without sitting back down beside me. "I'm sorry to cut this short, but there's something I need to do."

"Go ahead," I said without looking up at him.

"I'll catch up with you later?"

I saw from the corner of my eye that Tackle was looking at me, but I had no reason to catch up with him later or any other time.

"Bye," I said.

"You need…help?" Knox asked him.

"No, but thanks. I'll call you later."

9

Sloane

I managed to avoid Tackle throughout the rest of the holidays by staying at my friend's place in Boston. She was off on another trip, this time to Europe. I offered to sublet her apartment since I was staying there so often, but she laughed. "My dad owns the building, Sloane. It isn't like I pay rent."

This afternoon, I was on my way to Newton to say goodbye to Knox. He'd called earlier to say the missing-person case he was working on was taking him out of town. I'd told him I had to swing by the office first, but I hoped to be to him by noon or one.

"Thanks for driving over," he said when I walked into the house. "You didn't have to."

"I wanted to." I hugged him hard and looked down at his bag that sat at the bottom of the stairs.

"Can I give you a lift?"

"Nah, Tackle is on his way here now, but thanks."

I leaned forward and kissed his cheek. "I need to get back to work, but I wanted to see you. Stay safe and I love you."

Knox studied me in a way that made me uncomfortable. "I love you too, Sloane," he finally said.

Rather than return to the office right away, I stopped by the apartment to grab a bite to eat. While I didn't feel much better than I had on Christmas, I did find that if I ate small meals throughout the day, I didn't feel as nauseous. I'd decided earlier in the week that if my body didn't sort itself out by today, I'd make an appointment.

"Is there any chance you're pregnant?" the nurse at my doctor's office asked when I described my symptoms after sitting on hold for over twenty minutes.

"None."

"The first I can get you in to see a doctor is in two weeks. If you can't wait that long, you could always go to an urgent care facility."

I told her I could wait but if it got worse, that's what I'd do.

I gathered up what I needed for work, put my laptop in my bag, and took the elevator to the lobby. I stepped off, and my eyes met the very man I'd been trying to avoid. "What are you doing here?" I asked Tackle.

"I've been trying to connect with you for two weeks, Sloane. Longer than that, actually."

"Did it occur to you that I wasn't interested in connecting with *you*?"

"I've never known you to be rude."

"Too bad I can't say the same about you."

"Come on, Sloane. This conversation is long overdue."

"What it is, is unnecessary. There's nothing for us to talk about."

"I disagree. There are things I need to say."

I tried to step around him, but Tackle blocked me.

"Do you really want it to be this way between us?" he asked.

"Between us? There isn't any us. You're my brother's best friend. End of story. You've never needed to say anything to me in the past. You still don't."

"I want to explain."

"Leave me alone, Tackle."

He took a deep breath in and let it out slowly. "I'm begging. On your brother's life if I have to."

I was tempted to slap his fucking face. "Are you kidding me? Tell me you didn't just say that. How dare you?"

He hung his head. "I'm sorry. That was too much. It's just really important to me that we talk. Give me fifteen minutes. That's all I'm asking."

I looked at my phone as much to check the time as to buy myself a minute to think. The truth was, there wasn't much for me to do back at the office. At one point, I'd thought about taking the afternoon off.

"Fifteen minutes," I said. "That's it."

"Thank you."

We walked over to the elevator, and he pressed the call button. I couldn't help but remember the last time we were in the same place. I wanted so badly for him to kiss me like he had that day. Forget about talking. Fall into bed the second we walked through the door to the apartment.

When I looked up, Tackle was studying me. The moment our eyes met, he reached over and hit the emergency-stop button, bringing us to a jarring halt. His eyes still boring into mine, he crowded me into the corner.

"Tell me what you're thinking," he demanded.

I shook my head but didn't look away.

"About this?" He put his fingertips on my chin and kissed me exactly how he had that day.

Instead of stomping on his foot or biting his lip or kneeing him in the groin—I kissed him back. Not just that, I wrapped my arms around his neck.

"Once wasn't enough, Sloane. You know it as well as I do."

Like a bucket of ice water had been poured over me, the moment was ruined. I slid my hands from his neck to his chest and pushed with all my might. "*Stop this*," I spat.

His eyes opened wide. "I keep saying and doing the wrong thing when all I want to do is get it right."

"I can't be that person, Tackle. I can't scratch whenever you have an itch." I reached out and hit the emergency button again, and the elevator began moving.

"What makes you think that's what I want?"

I walked out when the door opened. "You said you wanted to explain, not ask me questions."

Tackle didn't speak again until we were inside the apartment. I pulled out a chair at the dining table and sat down. He did the same.

"That day on the staircase—I guess it was Christmas—you said something about me having a girlfriend. I don't."

"I don't care one way or the other," I lied.

"I know your brother told you there was a woman—"

"Like I said..."

He put his hand on the edge of my chair and turned it so we were sitting knee to knee. "You wanna know who I was talking about when I told your brother there was a woman who I wasn't sure felt the same way I did?"

"Absolutely not." I felt tears threatening. If I let myself cry now, it would be the most humiliating moment of my life.

"You."

"You're such a liar." I got up from the chair. Tackle stood too and grabbed my wrist.

"Look at me." He pulled me close to him, cupped my cheek with his palm, and stared into my eyes. "You, Sloane."

God, I wanted to believe him. Dare I?

"When that plane landed, there was a part of me that wished it was only you waiting for us. I even wished Halo wasn't with me. All I wanted to do was hold you in my arms and tell you..."

"Tell me what?"

"I've wanted you for years, Sloane. Even before I took you to your prom."

"You did that as a favor to Knox."

He shook his head. "Nope. Your mom called him and asked him to come home and take you. I told him I was going home anyway and volunteered to do it."

I scrunched my eyes. "What did Knox say?"

"He thanked me."

"Did he suspect anything?"

Tackle shook his head a second time.

I took a step back and folded my arms. "If he found out..."

"I know."

"So, why? Is this some sick 'you want me because you can't have me' thing?"

"No, Sloane."

I raised a brow. I'd buy that maybe I was the woman he'd been talking about. I'd also buy that he'd wanted me for a long time. I'd certainly wanted him long before my prom. But that didn't change the fact that Tackle was betraying my brother. We both were, but it felt worse to me that he was.

"We can't. Never again. Knox will never forgive us."

"Can you really walk away that easily?"

"Don't," I said when he took a step closer to me.

"You don't want me, Sloane? You don't want to feel me deep inside you? Feel my lips on you? My tongue?"

When his tone changed from needy to demanding, I wanted him so much more.

"Admit it."

How bad would it be if I just had sex with him one more time? The damage had already been done. Whether it happened once, twice, or ten times, Knox would still flip out. "I do," I whispered.

Tackle put one arm around me and kissed my neck. "From the time I woke up in the hospital in Columbia until our plane landed in DC, I've thought about this." He snaked his hand under my sweater and covered my breast with it. "And then you left before I could get a second taste."

He kissed me, hard and deep. His fingers toyed with my nipple. That alone made me feel like I was about to come out of my skin. My breasts were so sensitive I could barely stand his touch while, at the same time, every pinch was like a zinger straight to my clit.

"Do you know how I felt when I came out of the bathroom and you were gone?"

I shook my head, unable to think, let alone speak. When he pulled my sweater up, I lifted my arms so he could take it off. When he reached around, unfastened my bra, and removed it with his teeth, I swooned.

"You're not leaving again, Sloane. If I have to, I'll tie you to the bed until I've had my fill of you." He picked me up and carried me to the bedroom just like he had the first time. He kissed me, and I kissed him back—also in the same way we had that day.

He set me on the mattress, removed my boots, my socks, and finally, my pants. I lay there in nothing but my panties, watching him undress. Before taking off his jeans, he reached into his pocket and pulled out a handful of condoms.

"Pretty sure of yourself," I muttered.

Tackle dropped his pants and crawled onto the bed. "When it comes to you, Sloane, the last thing I am is sure of myself." He spread my legs and moved between them. "In fact, the only two things I'm sure of are how much I want you and how determined I am to get what I want."

When he moved my panties to the side and brought his mouth to my pussy, I jolted. I gripped his hair when he licked through my folds, and he looked up at me. "Sloane, has anyone done to you what I'm doing now?"

I raised my head to look at him and shook it.

"Good."

He took his time, swirling his tongue around and around my clit. When he sucked the hard little nub into his mouth, lightly nipping it with his teeth, then thrust two long fingers inside me and curled them, I went off like a rocket. "Oh my God," I screamed, unable to stop spasming as he drew out my orgasm until I thought I'd black out from pure ecstasy. My body shook with pleasure, not having realized anything could feel this wicked good.

He slowed his movements as though he was gently bringing me back down to earth. Somewhere in the back of my mind, I'd known Tackle would be an amazing lover. Maybe that was part of the reason I'd waited.

He moved up my body and brought his mouth to mine. I tried to turn my head away, but he held me still. "I want you to taste yourself on me, Sloane."

His kiss was gentle at first, but then became more heated as moans continued to emanate from my chest.

"I'm going to teach you to bring me pleasure with your mouth too, but not yet. First, I need to fuck you, Sloane. Do you want that?"

I nodded.

"Say it."

"I want it."

"Say the words like you did in the parking garage."

My cheeks flushed in embarrassment.

"Say it, Sloane," he repeated.

"I want you to fuck me, Tackle."

"How?"

"Fuck me hard."

He grabbed a condom, rolled it on, and knelt between my spread legs. "I could spend eternity inside your pussy. My tongue...my fingers...my cock." As he spoke the final two words, he positioned himself at my entrance and thrust into me. "God, you're so tight." He grabbed my legs and held them together so my ankles rested on his shoulder. When he pushed into me again, his eyes rolled back in his head.

I couldn't control all the sounds that seemed to come from somewhere deep in my throat of their own volition. When I put my hand over my mouth to stifle them, Tackle grabbed my wrist and moved it away. "I want to hear you."

A second orgasm overtook me, and this time, my cries turned into screams when he rubbed my clit and pounded into me.

Tackle pulled out, flipped me onto my stomach, and lifted me up on my knees. His hands gripped my waist as he continued his body's assault on mine.

"Come with me, Sloane," he growled. "I want to feel it."

As if I had any control over the orgasms he brought me to, but my body listened and did as he asked. His fingertips dug into my skin as he thrust one more time. I could feel him pulsing inside me.

He stilled and rolled us both to our sides, pulling my back flush with his front after he removed the condom. He moved my sweat-drenched hair and kissed the side of my face. "There's so much we need to talk about."

Like I'd had no control over my orgasms, I couldn't stop my body from stiffening with his words.

10

Tackle

"Not now," I said. "Now, we rest."

My guess was the one question she wouldn't want to answer was whether I was the first man she'd been with. Was there even a reason I needed to know? Other than how much it had turned me on when she confirmed that my mouth was the first to bring pleasure to her pussy. With that one thought, my cock stiffened.

I tightened my grip around her waist, moved her hair from her neck, and licked the moisture that coated her skin. Chill bumps covered her arms, and she shuddered.

"I really should—"

"Whatever you're about to say, Sloane, the answer is no."

"But I have to—"

"Do you? Really? Or are you just attempting to run like you did the first time?"

"You don't even know what I'm trying to say."

"Don't I? Are you about to lie and tell me you have to go back to work?"

"How do you know I'd be lying?"

"In the same way I knew every other time you lied in all the time I've known you."

"Maybe you don't know me as well as you think."

"Tell me the truth, Sloane. Do you have to go into work this late in the day on a Friday?"

"No."

"Since you were so sweet to tell me the truth, you deserve a reward." I shifted away from her and trailed kisses from her neck and all the way down her spine. When I made it to the dimples right above her ass, I reached between her legs and fingered the sweet pussy I was quickly growing addicted to. "I'm going to ask you another question, Sloane. If you tell me the truth, the rewards will keep right on coming."

"Can you just keep doing what you're doing and stop talking?"

I moved my hand away and rested it on her tummy.

"No," she groaned.

"No answers, no rewards."

"You're mean."

"But I can be very, very nice."

She huffed but then arched when I trailed my fingers back down to her pussy. "Ready?" I asked.

"For?"

"There's something I want to know, and I don't want you to lie to me."

"God, Tackle, just ask me, for fuck's sake."

I swatted her bottom, and she yelped. "I only want you to say that word when you're telling me how hard you want me to fuck you."

"Did you really just spank me?"

"First of all, that 'love tap' could hardly constitute a spanking." I put my fingers between her legs. "Second, tell me you didn't like it."

Her cheeks turned a bright shade of red, she looked away, and I moved my hand from her pussy to her hip.

"You're mean," she repeated, sticking her lower lip out.

"What I am is a man who wants to give you all the pleasure you can handle. I ask very little in return."

"What?"

"Do I want in return?"

She nodded.

"First, no matter what I ask, you answer truthfully."

"What else?"

"When we're together like this, naked, whatever I tell you to do, you do."

"What if I don't want to?"

I put my hand back between her legs and fingered her clit. "Then, you don't get this."

She was close; I could feel it. So when I took my hand away again, she cried out. "Stop teasing me."

"Do you promise to be honest with me?"

She looked over her shoulder and scowled at me. "Is this the method you use to get all women to talk?"

I massaged her ass where I'd swatted her earlier. "Don't ever say anything like that again. There aren't women; there's just you."

"Right."

That got her another swat.

She reached behind and rubbed her bottom, which brought the back of her hand in contact with my steel-hard cock. "Was there a question?" she muttered.

I put my mouth on her nape and sucked her flesh until I left a mark. "Was I your first, Sloane?" I tweaked her nipple when she didn't answer right away.

"Ouch!" She pushed my hand away. "That hurts."

"Answer me, Sloane."

"Yes!" she cried. "You were my first."

"Do you know how hard that makes me? How happy it makes me?"

"Where's my reward?" she whined and moved my hand away from her breast.

I grabbed another condom, rolled it on as fast as I could, and thrust into her from behind.

Within seconds, she was writhing against me and screaming my name along with God's. Oh, yeah, sex with Sloane was going to be all that I'd imagined and more. That she hadn't been with any other man before me made me want to pound my chest and roar.

"Where would you like to have dinner?"

Sloane's eyes met mine in the bathroom mirror. "Don't you have...things to do?" She turned around and tried to scoot by me, but I blocked her escape.

"Italian?"

"Tackle, please move."

"Not until you answer me."

"I'm not hungry."

I leveled my gaze at her and raised one eyebrow.

"Okay, jeez, I'm a *little* hungry." She stared into my eyes when we both heard my phone ringing in the other room. "Don't you need to get that?"

"Nope."

"What if it's work related?"

"It isn't."

"Maybe it's that woman."

I let her pass, and she went into the bedroom. I followed and watched as she got dressed and refused to make eye contact with me.

"Sloane, look at me."

She put her hands on her hips. "What?"

"Earlier, you said you couldn't be the person who scratched when I have an itch."

"That's right."

"Which means you want more."

"I never said that."

I walked over, grasped both her wrists, and put her hands on my hips. "How about we just start with a meal? Have dinner together?"

"Knox—"

"Is in New York City."

"How would he feel if he knew?"

I released her hands and sat down on the bed. "I've asked you to be honest with me, so I will answer truthfully. He wouldn't like it."

"And yet, you're still here. Still asking me to have dinner with you."

"I can't help it, Sloane. The idea that I could've died…it changed how I feel about things. How I think about them."

She sat beside me. "I get that."

"On our way back from Columbia, your brother asked if surviving the plane crash made me want to settle down, have kids, that kind of stuff."

"And?"

"I can't say I'll ever be ready to have kids. I mean, you know as well as I do how hard it is on the families with what I do for a living."

"You're going back to it?"

I shrugged. "It's too early for me to say for certain. My dad basically told me his business is mine if I want to take it over."

"But?"

"There was a reason I didn't go into construction and contracting to begin with. I don't know if I see myself doing that for the rest of my life either."

My phone rang again, and for the second time, I ignored it. I wished I'd thought to go turn it off before I followed Sloane in here.

"She's persistent," she mumbled.

"It's probably a spam call."

"Right." She smirked. "Back to what we were talking about. I didn't expect Knox to take on another mission so soon."

"I didn't either."

"You said that almost dying changed how you feel about things. What things?"

"Putting things off until tomorrow. Denying myself." I put my fingers on her chin and turned her head to look at me. "You."

"I don't know what that means."

"How about I tell you over dinner?"

"You aren't going to relent, are you?"

I shook my head. "I'm starving."

Sloane smiled. "I am too."

"There's a Moroccan place not too far from here."

"I know it. They started out with just a food truck. Now, it's one of the most popular restaurants in the city."

The place, located in the public market, was packed, but it didn't take us long to order and find a seat. Sloane got beet salad and a sweet lamb bowl while I chose the burnt-ends brisket bowl with couscous and roasted vegetables. We shared a cup of the best harissa soup I'd ever had while we waited for our entrées.

"I promised to tell you how the crash made me look at things differently."

Sloane's eyes met mine. "You did."

"I can't be passive anymore. I can't wait for things to happen. I mean, I can, but when I do, I get frustrated. I can't tell you how many times I found myself angry at not being able to talk to you. In the past, I would've let it go. Months could have gone by, and eventually, I would've given up."

"I'm sorry."

I reached over and ran my fingertip over the back of her hand. “I didn’t mean to make you feel bad. It’s all on me. What I can and can’t allow myself to do anymore.”

“Your life has been in danger before. How was this different?”

“The inevitability. In the past, there was always the chance that I’d overcome whatever obstacle was in front of me. It might mean I’d kill before I was killed or that I was rescued, like in Somalia. The plane going down, though, I didn’t think there was any chance we’d survive. The fact that we did, felt like a crazy miracle.”

Sloane moved her hand out from under mine and looked off in the distance. “What do you want from me, Tackle?”

“I want to spend time with you. I want to get to know who you are when you aren’t with your family.”

“I’m not different.”

“Yeah, you are. I’ve seen glimpses of it over the years. The night of the prom, the day our plane landed in DC. I saw the Sloane who isn’t just the daughter or the little sister. I want to know her better.”

“You said I know how hard the work you do can be on families. You’re right. I’ve seen it firsthand, both with you and Knox and with my dad. I’m not saying that you and I will ever be in a relationship, but the closer I get to you, the harder it will be every time I know you're out there, facing another dangerous situation." She took a deep breath and let it out slowly. "I worry about Knox so much."

"And you worry about me."

"Too much, Tackle. When your plane stopped on that tarmac, I wanted to see you more than my brother. I'm not sure either of my parents noticed, but I got the feeling your mother did."

"I think you're right. She said something about calling her that night if my plans changed. Since all I was supposedly doing was dropping you off at work, I thought her comment was odd."

"I'm not the kind of person who can hide what I'm feeling, Tackle. It could even be why I've felt nauseous for so many days in a row. It's like my body feels the subterfuge and wants to expel it."

"What are you feeling about me, Sloane?"

"The same things you are. The idea that you might have died without me knowing how it felt to be intimate with you was why I was, um, a little bolder than I've ever been."

Her cheeks turned pink, and she cast her gaze downward. Both things made my cock rock-hard. I held out my hand, and she put hers in it. "You asked what I wanted from you. I'm asking the same thing."

Sloane took a deep breath and let it out slowly. "This isn't easy to say, and I'd rather that after I have, you don't ask me any other questions."

"I can't make that promise."

"I didn't think so."

"Tell me anyway."

"I wanted you to be, you know, my first."

My already hard cock started to throb.

"That excites you?" she asked, perhaps noticing my accelerated breathing and the way I had to readjust my jeans.

"It does. Like you wouldn't believe."

She shrugged one shoulder. "We're done with that. You know and I know. We can check it off the list."

Her words caused an ache in my chest. "We've barely scratched the surface, Sloane."

My eyes met hers, challenging her to say otherwise. I never dreamed she would.

"I'm done, Tackle. I'm not interested in more."

I was stunned. "How can you say that?"

"I told you before, I can't be your hookup girl. It isn't who I am."

"We can do other things," I said, waving my free hand over the table. "Have dinner together. Hang out."

"Why?"

"Because I like you and you like me."

"No."

"Just like that? No?"

"We want different things in life."

"How do you know that?"

She laughed and folded her arms in front of her. "Whether you think so now or not, I can't imagine you won't, one day, go back to your job. That right there is enough for me to walk away."

I started to speak, but Sloane shook her head. "I want a regular life, Tackle. I'm hoping that now that I've gotten you out of my system, I can move on, find a nice guy, maybe even get married and start a family."

"No other man will make you feel as good as I can."

Sloane laughed. "You're right about me liking you. I do. I always have. Your cockiness, how you make me laugh, not to mention you have a killer body—"

"And I'm handsome."

She smirked. "Yes, you're handsome. All of that makes for a great crush. Even for the perfect person to finally give my virginity to. But not for real life. You know that as well as I do."

I wanted to argue, but could I? I knew Sloane was right. I wanted more time with her, but how much more? A couple of weeks where I spent as much time as I could with both of us naked, pleasuring each other's bodies? I said we could hang out, but eventually, that would get weird, and even though my friendship with Halo was strained presently, we'd still remain good friends—even best friends—for the rest of our lives. If things went on for too long between Sloane and me, maybe she'd start asking for more than I could give, and then it would be awkward between us forever.

"You're leaving me wanting more. I don't think anyone's ever done that before."

"It's good for you, Tackle. It'll build character."

"Is that what it'll do? I thought all I'd get out of it was a pair of blue balls."

Sloane laughed. "Let's walk away while we can still be friends. Okay?"

I nodded. "I don't like it, but you're right."

Sloane put her hand on her heart. "Did you just say I'm right? Wow, that plane crash really did change you."

11

Sloane

I let Tackle walk me back to my friend's building, but stopped short of inviting him up. If I did, we'd end up back in bed, and I couldn't do that. It didn't help his case that his phone rang two more times on the walk home, and instead of pulling it out, he ignored it.

"You sure about this?" he asked when we got to the elevator. "I could tuck you in."

"Tell you what, I'll go upstairs and you can return the call of whoever is so desperately trying to reach you."

He took a step forward, maybe to kiss me, but the elevator door opened and I stepped inside. "Goodbye, Tackle."

Walking away, hurt. I couldn't deny that, but I knew I had to make a clean break now, or when the time came that he did, I would be devastated.

While I didn't want kids right now, I knew that someday I would. When that time came, there was no way I could go through what my mother had when my father was gone for weeks at a time. I'd already experienced the bitter taste of worry too often.

On the elevator ride up, I thought about the wording of what I might say on a dating site. "Seeking a man who avoids danger and travel—a boring homebody."

I probably should add "really good at sex," since I knew it would be impossible for me not to compare every man I'd ever be with to Tackle. Something told me no man would ever measure up.

When I woke Saturday morning, I decided to pack up my stuff and go home. I could use a couple of days with my mother, letting her smother me in helicopter-mom overload.

I was just about to put on my jacket when I heard the intercom buzz. Other than on the rare occasion I ordered food delivery, I never heard it. And since I wasn't expecting anyone, I ignored it.

The thing rang again as I walked out the door and locked it behind me. Once in the elevator, I stuck a ball cap on my head, fastened my jacket up tight to my neck, and wrapped a scarf around the lower part of my face.

With my duffel bag slung over my shoulder, I stepped off in the lobby. Wait. The *lobby*? I meant to go to the lower parking level. I turned around to get back on the elevator, but the door had already closed.

I felt someone's hand on my shoulder at the same time I heard Tackle's voice say, "Let me get that for you."

I spun around, tightening my grasp on my bag. "What are you doing here?"

"I was hoping to take you out for breakfast, but thought I'd either missed you or you were still asleep."

"*Breakfast*? No. Last night we agreed—"

"To remain friends."

I pulled him over to the side when one of the other tenants approached the elevator.

"To remain what we were. You're my older brother's best friend. That's it. We weren't friends, Tackle."

He shook his head. "Nope. This is what you said, 'Let's walk away while we can still be friends.' Those were your exact words."

"You knew what I meant."

"Sure did. So here I am, inviting my friend out for breakfast."

I stared up into his big green eyes, wondering if there would ever come a time I could say no to this man and actually mean it.

"Come on, you know you're hungry."

I was, actually. More, I was beginning to feel a little nauseous. If I didn't eat something soon, it might get worse. "Breakfast, and then I have to head home."

"Not a problem. I'll be happy to drop you off."

"What? No. Tackle, you can't drop me off."

"Of course I can."

I folded my arms. "And what do you expect me to tell my mother when she sees your car?"

"Tell her I was in the city anyway, so I offered you a ride."

"That makes zero sense. I have my car and—"

"Can we eat first and argue about how you're going to get home later?"

I rolled my eyes. "Sure."

Tackle took the bag off my left shoulder, slung it over his, and then held my hand with his right one.

"Friends don't hold hands."

"Oh yes, they do. Haven't you ever seen Halo and me? We hold hands all the time."

"You're such a weirdo."

"You love that about me."

That was almost enough for me to wrench my hand from his. Yes, I did love that about him. Just like I loved everything about Tackle Sorenson.

He dropped my hand and put his arm around my shoulders. "Don't freak out, peanut. I was just joking. Friends don't love friends, right?" Before I could answer, he winked. "Or do they?"

After breakfast, he talked me into going shopping with him. "While I survived the plane crash, the clothes I took with me to South America didn't. I need to replenish."

We'd just stepped out of the department store's revolving door when I heard Tackle's cell vibrate. Like every other time he received a call when he was with me, he ignored it. On one hand, I could look at it as him being polite. On the other, I couldn't help but wonder what he was hiding. Every time I insisted he just answer the damn thing, he ignored me, so I didn't bother repeating it. Until, less than five minutes later, while we were in the men's department, looking at shirts, it happened again.

"That's it," I said, setting the button-down shirt I had in my hand back on the display table. "I'm going home."

When I walked away, he grabbed my arm. "Wait. Why?"

"You don't even take it out to see who it is, which to me, means you don't want to risk my seeing it either."

"I don't check, because I know it isn't important."

"How do you know?"

"Tell me you don't have certain ringtones for certain people or types of calls."

"I do, but your phone didn't ring; it just vibrated."

Tackle sighed and pulled the phone out of his pocket. "Look," he said. "Unknown number."

"But you didn't know that." I kept walking to the store's exit.

"Tell you what, if I get another call, I won't ignore it."

I shook my head. "We shouldn't be doing this anyway."

"Doing what?"

"Hanging out. I made myself clear last night, Tackle."

The playful look on his face turned into a scowl, or was it a pout? He put his hand on my shoulder, then slid it to the back of my neck. When he brought his forehead to mine, I almost wrapped my arms around his waist. "Sloane," he murmured right before brushing my lips with his. "Please."

I pulled back. "Please, what? What are you asking of me?"

"I don't know exactly. All I do know is that I can't stay away from you. Whatever it takes, I'll do. Just please don't kick me out of your life."

Even when he was being a jerk, I couldn't say no to him. When he was sweet—vulnerable—like he was now? There was no way I could deny him. I sighed. "This is a bad idea."

When his look changed to hopeful, I wanted to slug him. "Do you always get your way?"

He shook his head. "If I did, I would've woken up this morning with you naked beside me."

"Tackle—"

He held up one hand. "Honesty, remember? I'm not going to lie and say I don't want to kiss you right now, but I will resist since I know it isn't what you want."

I brought my lips to his in a chaste kiss and then twisted out of his hold. "Come on, let's finish shopping. I'm getting hungry again."

12

Tackle

After we ate a late lunch and went back to Sloane's friend's apartment, she decided to take a nap before driving to her parents' house.

"I don't know why I'm so tired," she mumbled when I lay down on the bed, beside her. She yawned and rolled to her side. "You don't have to stay."

I went out to the living room and grabbed a throw I'd noticed on the back of the sofa. In the short time it took me to do that, Sloane had fallen fast asleep. I covered her with the blanket and lay back down beside her.

As much as I wanted to touch her, caress her cheek, I didn't want to wake her, so I kept my hands to myself and thought about our conversation from earlier in the day. "What are you asking of me?" she'd said. I didn't have a good answer then or now. I knew this, though. If Sloane wasn't Halo's younger sister, I'd want to date her, see where that took us. At the very least, spend a few months enjoying each other's company and bodies.

Would the fact that her brother was my best friend really preclude that? He might be uncomfortable at first, maybe even angry, but he'd get over it.

It was what happened after the relationship ended that worried me more. If I hurt Sloane, if she wanted more than I was prepared to give, it might end more than my friendship with Halo. What about our parents? They'd become good friends too. Was spending time with her worth the risk? If we could stay friends, it would be.

I tucked my arms under my head and stared up at the ceiling, jolting when Sloane turned and snuggled her body close to mine. She murmured words I couldn't understand, but she looked content, peaceful. I put my arm around her and kissed the top of her head.

There wasn't another woman I wanted to be with, liked more, was attracted to in the same way I was to Sloane.

She'd also asked if I always got my way. Most of the time, yes. I also worked hard to build the life I wanted for myself. When I closed my eyes, I could envision us together. That should scare the shit out of me. Instead, it filled me with an inexplicable warmth.

"What time is it?" Sloane asked, rolling to her back and stretching her arms above her head.

I had no idea except that the sun was setting.

She pulled out her phone. “I can’t believe I slept for three hours.” She turned her head toward me. “You didn’t have to stay.”

“I fell asleep too.” I stretched like she had and then rubbed my belly. “I can’t believe I’m hungry again.”

Sloane laughed. “I’m so glad you said it first.”

“What sounds good? We could order takeout, or I could run to the market and make us something.”

When she didn’t answer, I turned my body toward hers.

“I’ve decided you’re a figment of my imagination.”

I laughed like she had. “Why?”

“First, Tackle Sorenson is lying next to me, on a bed no less. Second, you just offered to cook food for me.”

“Neither should surprise you that much.”

“No?” She tapped her cheek with her finger. “If a year ago, someone had predicted this was where you’d be on a Saturday night, would you have believed them?”

“Probably not.”

She rolled onto her back and looked up at the ceiling. “What are we doing?” she groaned.

“Trying to decide what to have for dinner.”

“You know what I mean.”

“How about this? Instead of talking so much about why we’re spending time together, why don’t we just enjoy it?”

"My gut is telling me that isn't a good idea, but it's also telling me I'm hungry."

"Takeout would be faster."

"I'm glad you said that first too."

We settled on Chinese since there was a place Sloane liked just down the street. Rather than using plates, we passed the containers back and forth, digging in with chopsticks.

"Don't bogart the shrimp, Tackle," she said, grabbing the container from my hand.

"Bogart? You're as bad as Halo."

As soon as the words were out of my mouth, I wished I hadn't said her brother's name. The smile left her face, and she set the container on the table.

"Don't," I muttered, knowing that no matter what I said, she was about to go down the "we shouldn't be doing this" road again.

She drummed her chopsticks on the table. "So what's the deal with Ghafor?" she asked instead.

"Whoa. That was out of left field."

"I know, right? I've been wondering about him, though. He seems to have fallen off the radar."

"The good news is, the agency has him under their thumb. The bad news is, guys like him don't stay there long."

In mid-December, the mission that took Halo and me to Columbia had culminated with the assassination of the Russian-backed then-president of the country, Petro Santos, and the reinstatement of the US-backed former president, Francisco Marquez.

Abdul Ghafor, leader of the Islamic State, had played an integral role in making that happen by way of the CIA. Even though the Middle East was my area of expertise, knowing what he got in exchange was above my pay grade.

As I'd said, a man as evil and ruthless as Ghafor certainly wouldn't remain loyal to the United States any longer than it served his organization's—or his—purposes.

"Where is he? Do you know?" Sloane asked.

"If I had to guess, I'd say Pakistan. Is he on your watch list?"

"I monitor cells in the northeast region. His name comes up every now and then."

"I haven't been briefed on the details of how everything played out, but I'm sure you watched it unfold the same as I did."

She nodded. "Columbia may be stable for now, but I wouldn't predict it will last long." Sloane picked up the shrimp and took a few bites. "Gotta tell you, I'm happy I work for DHS."

"Me too."

She studied me. "Why?"

"You think you worry about Halo and me? I can't imagine how bad we'd be if you'd gone into international intelligence."

"It isn't like my assignments are danger-free, Tackle. I am a criminal investigator."

"Thanks for reminding me." I ran my hand over my hair, which was due for a buzz cut.

"Don't be a hypocrite."

I reached over and put my other hand on hers. "I can't help it, Sloane, any more than you can flip a switch on worrying about me, your brother, or even your dad."

As if on cue, my cell phone vibrated. While sometimes I could turn it off, I didn't like to do so very often in case it was someone from K19, my parents, or now, Halo, since he was on assignment. Instead, I blocked Nick's number, knowing I'd done as much as I could for her given the circumstances.

"Answer it or leave," said Sloane, getting up from the table.

"That's kind of harsh."

She leaned up against the kitchen counter and folded her arms. "My borrowed apartment, my rules."

I dug the phone out, not thrilled when I saw it was a number I didn't recognize. Hiding something or not, I never answered those.

"Sloane—"

"You heard me, Tackle."

I hit the accept button. "Sorenson."

"Tackle, finally, I've been trying to get a hold of you." Nick sounded out of breath but was talking loudly enough that there was no way Sloane hadn't heard every word she said.

"I need to call you back."

"Wait! Don't hang up. I can't stay here. You need to come and get me."

"I'll call you back, Nick."

"Time to say good night," said Sloane, cleaning up the remnants of our dinner.

"There was a reason I told Nick I needed to call her back, and it isn't because I don't want you to hear what I have to say."

"Or her?"

"Can we sit?"

"Whatever you need to say—" Sloane clapped her hand over her mouth and raced off in the direction of the bathroom. Not knowing what else to do, I followed and stood outside the door when she slammed it closed. I leaned up against the wall and waited. I moved a couple of feet away when I heard the water running in the sink. Seconds later, she came out, wiping her hands on a towel.

"Is there anything I can do?"

She shook her head. "I'm going to bed." When I followed again, Sloane stopped at the room's doorway. "Tackle, you need to leave."

I reached out and felt her forehead. "No fever."

"You sound like my mother."

"I'm worried about you, Sloane. You've been sick since Christmas."

"I have a doctor's appointment scheduled."

"When?"

She glared at me, put one hand on her hip, and pointed toward the door with the other.

"I'll sleep on the sofa, but I'm not leaving."

"I want to be left alone."

I rested my arm on the doorjamb. "I can always call Mama Clarkson."

"You wouldn't dare."

I pulled out my phone.

"What about your other phone call? You promised *Nick* you'd call her back."

"That can wait."

"Of course it can. Just leave, Tackle. *Leave.* I'm not kidding."

"Right." I dropped my arm, put it behind her knees, and swept her up. I took two steps into the room and gently rested her on the bed. "I'm not going anywhere, but I will leave you alone. As I said, I'll sleep on the sofa." I brushed her hair from her forehead and softened the tone in my voice.

13

Sloane

"Just let me..."

I couldn't tear my eyes away from Tackle's. "Just let you, what?"

"Stay. Worry about you. Be here if you need anything."

I should stand my ground; the truth was, I didn't have the energy to. I'd asked him—told him—to leave, and he continued to refuse. Telling him again now wouldn't be any different. He'd still stay.

"Okay."

"Okay, I can stay?"

"As if you wouldn't, no matter what I said."

He smiled. "Let's get you tucked in." He pulled the covers back on one side of the bed and told me to roll over before doing the same on the other side.

"Thanks," I murmured.

"Good night, then." He turned to leave the room.

"Tackle?"

"Yeah?"

"You could stay. I mean, here, in the bedroom."

"Are you sure you wouldn't sleep better without me in bed beside you?"

I smiled. "I think I can resist the temptation."

He smiled too and winked. "I'm not sure I can, but I'll do my best."

When he undressed and got in bed next to me, I looked into his mesmerizing green eyes. The features of his face were as perfect as the body he worked so hard to maintain. My eyes trailed down to his bare chest, and I squeezed my thighs together.

It didn't matter that I'd just lost the contents of my stomach; I wanted Tackle to remove his boxer briefs, the only thing he'd left on, and feel him inside me.

"You keep looking at me that way, and there's no way I'll be able to resist the temptation."

"I don't want you to."

He took a deep breath, closed his eyes, and slowly opened them. "I told you I'd leave you alone so you could rest."

"There's something I want more than sleep."

Tackle studied me but didn't move a muscle.

"Unless you don't want to."

When he raised the sheet, I saw that he did, in fact, want to very much. I reached out and grasped his cock when he lowered his briefs. He hissed a breath in.

"You have no idea how many times I imagined this."

"Did you, really?"

"Oh, yeah," he groaned.

"What else did you imagine?"

"How it would feel to have your mouth on me."

I scooted my body down the bed, rested one hand on his hip, and swirled my tongue on the tip of his cock. Tackle wove his fingers in my hair.

"Open, drop your hands, and hold still." His hands were on both sides of my face. He slowly eased farther into my mouth. "Deeper, Sloane. Relax your throat." When I gagged, he pulled out of my mouth and moved his hands from my head. "Jesus, I'm sorry. You were just sick."

He rolled out of bed and grabbed his clothes.

"Where are you going?"

"Into the other room."

When I woke the next morning and went out to the kitchen, it was clean, but Tackle was gone. I told myself it was for the best; I'd been trying to get him to leave anyway. Neither thought made the ache of missing him hurt less.

I called my mom and asked if there was anything she wanted me to pick up for her on my way home. I hurriedly jotted down the grocery list she rattled off.

"I thought you were coming yesterday, *mija*."

I told her I'd ended up running errands in the city, and by the time I got back to the apartment, I was too tired to make the drive.

"I'm worried about you."

"I made a doctor's appointment, but if you want me to wait to find out if whatever I have is contagious, I can stay here."

"Don't be ridiculous. Come home, Sloane. If you don't feel like stopping at the market, your father can go."

I laughed, thinking about the number of times my dad would have to call my mom when he couldn't find whatever she wanted. "I can do it."

I packed up my clothes, also known as laundry, grabbed my computer, and took the elevator down to the parking garage. Just that, made me think about Tackle and how I wished he hadn't left.

"So stupid," I mumbled and shook my head as I loaded my stuff into the backseat of my car. I'd lost count of how many times I repeated those words in my head at the grocery store and out loud as I drove to my parents' house.

When I came to the Newton town line, I thought about driving by Tackle's house, but what if he saw me? How embarrassing would that be?

Instead, I stepped on the gas, hoping to catch the stoplight before it turned red. There were two reasons I wanted to. The first was that it always felt like a ten-minute wait before it changed to green again. The second was that the grill was on the right side of the intersection. I tried not to look, but when the light changed and I was stuck there, I couldn't stop myself. I thought about how I'd picked up Tackle and my brother there on Christmas night.

I was about to turn away when I saw Tackle's car pull in and park next to the only other one in the lot. The car behind me honked as I watched him get out and greet the woman who had gotten out of the car next to him.

I drove away but could still see in the rearview mirror when he embraced the woman my brother had referred to as *Nick*.

"What's wrong, *mija*?" my mother asked when I slammed one of the bags of groceries down on the kitchen counter.

"Nothing."

She raised a brow.

"You know how much I hate traffic."

"There was traffic on a Sunday?"

Actually, there hadn't been. In fact, I was one of the only cars on the road. Except for Tackle and his *girlfriend*. I growled at the reminder and then realized my mother was studying me.

"You are acting very strange."

I shrugged. "I am strange, Mom." I put my arm around her shoulders and kissed her cheek. "Are you just figuring that out?"

"Sit and talk to me," she said, pointing to the table. I spent the rest of the afternoon with her in the kitchen while she cooked and insisted on doing my laundry for me.

"You aren't going back into the city tonight," she said, not phrasing it as a question.

I hadn't planned on it, so I didn't argue.

She, my father, and I were just finishing dinner when my mother got up and looked out the window.

"What?" I asked when her brow furrowed.

"Tackle is here."

While my father got up and answered the door, I went in the opposite direction and ran up the back stairs to my bedroom. "Bathroom," I shouted behind me when my mother asked where I was going.

To stop myself from listening to hear if he asked for me, or worse, giving in to the urge to go downstairs and confront him, I ran a bath, undressed, and climbed in before I could change my mind.

I don't know how much time had passed when I heard a knock at the bathroom door. "Sloane?" my mother called out when I didn't answer.

"Yeah?"

"Are you okay?"

"Fine, Mom."

"So strange," I heard her mutter as she walked away.

The next morning, my father and I drove into the city together since he had meetings all day at the State Department field office, located in the same building as DHS.

"Seems you have a lot on your mind, peanut."

As with *everything* else that could be remotely linked to my brother's best friend, his use of the nickname Knox had given me and Tackle had taken up using regularly made my heart ache all over again. Not that it had ever really stopped.

"Anything I can help with?"

"It's nothing," I said, looking out the passenger-side window.

"Work related?"

"Have you heard anything about Abdul Ghafor? I mean, anything you can tell me?"

"Funny you should ask. Tackle is coming in for a meeting today on the same subject."

I spun my head and gaped. "Are you serious? Why?"

"Probably for the same reason you asked about him."

"I was curious. That's different than having a meeting."

"You're welcome to join us."

"Thanks, but no thanks, Dad."

He glanced over at me. "It's at thirteen hundred hours if you change your mind."

"Thanks," I repeated.

"You're welcome," he said again, not realizing what I'd offered my appreciation for was that I now knew exactly at what time I'd be heading out for lunch.

***

"Hey."

I groaned when I heard Tackle's voice just as I was about to get into my car. "What?" I said without turning around to look at him. I jerked away when I felt his hand on my shoulder.

"I've been trying to get a hold of you."

"Why?"

"Sloane. Look at me."

Instead, I got in the car. He grabbed the door before I could close it.

"Leave me alone, Tackle," I snapped.

"Hot and cold much?"

"Are you fucking kidding me? You're accusing *me* of running hot and cold? That's rich."

"Yeah, I am. One minute, you're sucking my cock, and the next, you're blocking my calls again."

"You're such an asshole. Let go of the door."

"No. I want some answers. Are you seriously pissed because I left Sunday morning?"

"Not at all. I was glad you were gone."

"Is it because I was gentleman enough to get out of bed when I knew you didn't feel well?"

"Here's the deal, Sorenson. I'm not pissed. In fact, I couldn't care less if I ever see or talk to you again."

"I don't believe that shit for a hot minute."

"Again, I don't care." I pulled my phone out. "Either let go, or I'll call security."

He took a step back. "We're not finished," I heard him say before I slammed the door.

"Oh yes, we are," I responded, not caring whether he could hear me or not. I put the car in gear and pulled out of the space. This time when I looked in the rear-view mirror, instead of seeing him hugging another woman, I saw a very angry man.

14

Tackle

If there were a playbook for how not to handle things with Sloane, I was following all the don'ts to the letter.

First, I'd left Sunday morning without waking her to tell her or even leaving a note. Why? Because I figured it would be easier than lying to her when she asked where I was going.

Then I stopped by her parents' house and when her mother said that it sounded as though Sloane had started to run a bath, came up with the lame excuse that I wanted to have a meeting with her father about Abdul Ghafor. Now, here I was, with no real reason for wanting to meet, after having managed to piss Sloane off even more.

This was why I didn't do relationships. Trying to spend time with someone on a regular basis was more damn trouble than it was worth. And Sloane? God, I couldn't keep up with her mood swings. I probably shouldn't have said the thing about her sucking my cock, but it was true. One second, she wanted me, the next, she didn't.

If this were any other woman, she would never hear from me again. Literally. But this was Sloane, and no matter how hard I tried, I couldn't stay away. Even now, in the back of my mind, I was trying to come up with another way to get her to talk to me.

And then there was Nick. If only Sloane wanted me the way Nick did, the tables sure would turn. I'd be sick of her in a hot minute.

The only reason I'd agreed to meet with the other woman in person was to get her off my ass and convince her to leave me out of her fucked-up life. Instead of achieving either of those things, I seemed to have made Nick more determined than ever to spend every moment she could with me.

Kind of like I was being with Sloane. Jeez. Was it the same? Was I as annoying?

Whereas five minutes ago I was pissed, now I felt like a complete jackass. I walked over to the elevator, hoping that by the time I met with Mr. Clarkson, I would be able to get his daughter out of my head long enough to invent a reason for requesting the meeting in the first place.

When I walked into the conference room where the meeting was scheduled, I was surprised to find the only person there was Sloane's father.

"Are we expecting anyone else?" I asked after we'd made small talk for several minutes.

Mr. Clarkson shook his head. "I do understand you wanted to discuss Ghafor, but I have other things I'd like to talk over with you."

"Of course, sir."

"Tackle, I consider you part of our family..."

Jesus, was he about to say something about Sloane? Had she gone to him for help getting me to leave her alone? If so, I could see my relationship with the entire Clarkson family ending here and now.

He cleared his throat. "I want you to know you can come to me anytime. If you need a sounding board to help you figure out whether you're ready to go back to work with K19, I'd be happy to lend an ear."

"I appreciate that, sir."

"I'm going to give you some unsolicited advice, if that's okay with you."

"Of course," I repeated.

"If I had it to go back and do over, I'd change a lot of things about my life."

"You would?"

He nodded. "I'm not sure I'd even work for the State Department."

"No?"

"If I did, I would insist on a job that allowed me to stay home more. It was very hard on Carolina and the kids with me gone most of the time. My wife begged me to dissuade Knox from working for the agency, but I felt I had to respect the decisions he made for his own life."

"Have you told him what you're telling me now?"

"I did, right before he left. I sense, though, that you and he may be at very different places in your lives."

"What makes you say that?"

"The simplest answer is by the way you came straight back to Massachusetts after your Columbian ordeal while he chose to stay with your teammate in DC."

Here I was, the man who avoided confrontation at any cost, charging straight into the midst of it. "And the more complicated answer?"

Mr. Clarkson sat back in his chair but rested his palms on the edge of the table. "I'd say you know better than I do."

There was no doubt in my mind that he was referring to what was happening between Sloane and me. However, it didn't sound as though he necessarily disapproved. The words of wisdom he gave me could also be construed as words of warning. If I was in a relationship with his daughter, then I should make note of the fact that if he could do it over again, he wouldn't choose a life that took him away from home.

But we weren't in a relationship. In fact, she told me straight out that she never wanted to see me again. I didn't believe her, but even then, what was between us wouldn't constitute anything more than casual dating coupled with equally casual sex.

If I wanted to walk out of here alive, I couldn't tell him that.

"Now, should we talk about Abdul Ghafor?"

"I'm looking to get information more than give it."

Mr. Clarkson smiled. "I gathered as much." He reached over and picked up a manila envelope. "This is what we know."

I wouldn't disrespect the man by asking if he remembered I was no longer employed by the agency. At the same time, I was stunned by his lack of propriety, given what he handed me was highly classified information.

"Thank you, Mr. Clarkson, sir."

"Don't you think it's time you started calling me Benjamin? Like I said, I consider you practically part of our family."

I left the DHS offices knowing what I'd just experienced was Benjamin Clarkson proving his trust in me. Was it a challenge? Was he saying he trusted me enough to break State Department protocol and, therefore, expected me to understand he was trusting me to do the right thing when it came to his daughter? Or was all of that bullshit I'd concocted by way of a guilty conscience?

When I left the office, I didn't go straight to the parking garage. Instead, I went for a walk. Fifteen minutes later, I sat in the café across the street from Sloane's friend's apartment, wondering why in the hell I was there.

15

Sloane

"He left about ten minutes ago," said my father when I answered his call.

"What are you talking about?"

"You know exactly what I'm talking about—the man you hightailed it out of here today to avoid in the same way you raced up the back staircase when he showed up at the house yesterday."

"Dad, I—"

"Stop right there. I haven't decided whether I want to know what's going on between the two of you, but based on your behavior and his, I know there's something."

"What do you mean by his behavior?"

"Sloane, do you know what you're doing?"

It took me a long time to answer, and even after I decided to tell him the truth, I wasn't sure I should. "No, Dad, I don't."

"I'm going to give you a piece of advice."

"Okay."

"Life speeds by far more quickly than you think it will at your age. One day, you'll wake up and be my age, and I hope, unlike me, you don't wish you'd done things differently."

"What does that mean? What do you wish you'd done differently?"

"That seems obvious, Sloane. I wish I wouldn't have put the job before my family. But I'm not saying your reason for regret would be the same as mine. What I'm suggesting is you make sure that when you *are* my age, you don't wish you would've taken the chances you're trying to talk yourself out of."

"What about Knox?"

"He must think Tackle is a decent guy to have remained friends with him all these years."

"What if this makes him change his mind?"

"Like I said, peanut, think long and hard whether you want to walk away without taking a chance."

"What if he doesn't want to take a chance with me?"

"You're a smart woman whose only reason for asking such a question is based on your own insecurity."

"Thanks, Dad."

"I'm going to take the train home tonight."

"You don't mind?"

"Not in the least."

I walked over to the window and thought about everything my father had said. I couldn't help but wonder if he and my mom had talked about Tackle and me.

Most likely not, since she wouldn't have hesitated to harangue me about him if they had.

Just as I was going to walk back into the kitchen, I saw Tackle go inside the café across the street. I stayed where I was and watched him take a table near the front window. I took a step back, hoping that, if he looked up, he wouldn't see me.

I'd told my dad I didn't know what I was doing. Did Tackle? Was he as confused about this as I was? I assumed I was only a notch in his bedpost, but if that were the case, why was he being so persistent? Because I was a challenge? And what was the deal between him and Nick?

There was only one way for me to get the answers. I grabbed my jacket and raced down the stairs rather than wait for the elevator, hoping he hadn't left.

He looked up as I waited for the light to change to cross the street, and while our eyes met, he didn't otherwise acknowledge I was headed his way.

I walked inside and told the hostess I was meeting the man seated near the window. The man who stood and pulled a chair out for me when I approached.

"Hi, Tackle."

"Hello, Sloane."

"We need to talk."

"I agree."

"My dad knows there's something going on between us."

He nodded slowly. "I wondered if you told him."

"I didn't."

He studied me for a few seconds.

"He said he figured there was, based on your behavior and mine."

Tackle leaned forward and rested his elbows on the table. "How did you respond?"

"Not with much, other than to answer honestly when he asked if I knew what I was doing. I told him I didn't." I waited for him to say something, but he remained silent. "Do you know what you're doing, Tackle?"

He leaned back in his chair and looked left and right. "No fucking clue."

"Why are you here?"

"I can't answer that either. I wish I could."

"My dad told me to think long and hard about whether I wanted to walk away without taking a chance."

"A chance at what?"

I cocked my head. He was the one who had been in such hot pursuit of me. Now, he was playing dense? "I'm sure he meant a chance at having more sex." I was so tempted to get up and leave. I closed my eyes and silently counted to five. If Tackle didn't speak by the time I did, I wouldn't just walk out. I'd go back to the office and put in for a transfer out of the Boston office to a place far enough away that I'd never have to see my brother's best friend again.

"Listen, Sloane..."

"You have ten seconds to finish that sentence."

"I like you. I always have. And to be completely honest, I've wanted to have sex with you since you were old enough for me to think about it without feeling like a pedophile."

"I can't believe this."

"Let me finish."

I stood. "Not necessary. I get it. The reason you've wanted so desperately to talk to me was only so you could be the one to give me the brush-off. Fuck you, Tackle." I raced out of the restaurant and into the cab that someone had just gotten out of.

"Where to?" the driver asked as he pulled away from the curb.

"Somewhere that will get me back here in no less than fifteen minutes."

"How 'bout Fenway?"

"Perfect."

When we pulled up across the street from the café twenty minutes later, I made sure Tackle wasn't still sitting at the table by the window before I got out. I reached into my pocket to pay the fare, realizing then that I'd left the apartment without my wallet.

"I'll be back in two minutes," I told the driver after apologizing. "Keep the meter running."

He nodded, and I got out, hoping Tackle wasn't waiting for me inside the building. I didn't see a single other person in the lobby while I waited for the elevator or when I came back downstairs after grabbing my wallet. I rushed out the door and didn't see the cab either.

"Shit," I muttered, looking left and right. "Where did he go?"

"If you mean the cabbie, he got another fare," said a woman waiting a few feet away at the bus stop.

"I owed him money," I mumbled.

"Whoever the guy was must've really needed to get somewhere quick cause I heard him say he'd take care of it."

"Was he about this tall?" I raised my hand in the air. "Short hair and wearing a brown leather jacket?"

"Sounds about right."

The bus pulled up, and she got on before I could ask anything else. "Thanks," I called out after her.

By the time I got back upstairs to the apartment, the nausea I'd felt on and off for the last few weeks had returned. I peeled a banana, hoping I could get it down before I felt worse. After inhaling it, I went into the bedroom, intending to put the rest of my things into a bag and go home. Instead, I lay on the bed, buried my face in the pillow, and cried.

***

The time between my telling Tackle to fuck off and the day of my doctor's appointment passed uneventfully. I went to work, came back to the apartment, and went home to my parents' house, all without him showing up or me running into him.

I left his number blocked so I wouldn't know whether he tried to call or not, yet thought of little else besides him.

While I wasn't so sick that I thought it warranted a visit to urgent care, the nausea came and went enough that I knew something had to be wrong with me.

The nurse had called to say they wanted to draw blood, so I had to fast prior to my appointment. Fortunately, I was able to go in at seven and get it done. I always felt worse if I didn't eat a decent breakfast.

Six hours later, I was ushered into a room and asked to strip down and put on one of those horrid hospital gowns that no one could ever get fastened in the back.

I grabbed my jacket and put it around my shoulders so I could stay warm in the chilly room. Ten minutes later, I heard a knock at the door, and the doctor came in, followed by a nurse.

She rolled a stool close to me while the other woman opened up a laptop and stood near her.

"You're worrying me," I said, wringing my hands.

"We were able to get the results of your blood and urine tests from this morning, and there is nothing for you to worry about. However"—the nurse handed the doctor the laptop—"you said twice that there was no way you could be pregnant."

"That's right."

"I had the lab run the tests more than once, just to be certain. Both returned the same results. You are pregnant, Miss Clarkson."

"That can't be," I whispered, gripping both sides of the exam table when vertigo overcame me.

The doctor put her hand on one of mine. "Evidently, this is a surprise to you."

"I only..." Had sex a couple of times? Was that what I was about to tell her? My eyes filled with tears, and I buried my face in my hands.

This couldn't be happening. I'd saved myself until I was twenty-six fucking years old, and I got pregnant the first damn time I had sex? What were the odds? I dropped my hands and laughed, maniacally, but it was still laughter.

"What is your relationship with the father?" the doctor asked.

"Nonexistent."

"I apologize if this feels intrusive, but do you know who the father is?"

Through more maniacal laughter, I answered. "Oh, yes."

"I'd like to perform an exam, after which we can discuss the next steps."

As she poked, prodded, and pressed on different parts of my body, the doctor asked if I recalled when my last menstrual cycle was. I did, and it was before Thanksgiving, I realized as tears rolled down the side of my face. That hadn't occurred to me until now? God, I was such an idiot.

"You can sit up," the doctor said, holding out her hand to help me. "Based on the timing of your last period and other indicators, I'd say you're still in your first trimester. You do have options."

"What options?" Abortion? Was that what she was suggesting?

"I can't help but notice you don't seem happy about the news. I'd like to refer you to an OB/GYN who can discuss them with you. In the meantime, take this pamphlet home with you and think things over."

Before leaving, the woman at the front desk scheduled an appointment for me to see the other doctor on Monday, giving me the weekend to "think things over."

Earlier in the day, I'd told my mother to expect me home this weekend, so the first thing I did when I returned to my friend's apartment was to call and tell her that something had come up and I'd be staying in the city after all.

"Is everything okay, *mija*?"

"Yes, fine," I lied. "I had something come up that I need to take care of." That was certainly the truth.

I spent the entire weekend alternating between crying and throwing up. Sometimes at the same time. By Sunday, I'd worked myself up into such a tizzy that I had to talk to someone.

Who, though? My mother? No way. My father? That would be worse, especially given the bizarre conversation he and I had had. I had a few friends from work, but the last thing I would tell any of them was that I was pregnant. Same with friends from school. If I did that, word would spread in our town like wildfire.

There was only one person I could trust not to say a word to anyone—Knox. And he was on a mission. But hadn't he and Tackle both said it was a missing-person case? That had to mean there was less risk involved, right? It wasn't like he was undercover somewhere.

"Hey, Sloane. Everything okay?"

While I'd vowed not to cry, the minute I heard my brother's voice, I dissolved into sobs so intense I couldn't speak.

"Sloane?" he said in a raised voice. "Is it something with Mom or Dad?"

"No, I'm sorry." I blew my nose.

"What's wrong?"

"I just...I need...I'm sorry."

"Sloane, I can hardly hear you."

"Is there...any...way...you can...come home? I know I'm asking a lot, but I need you, Knox."

"You're breaking up again, but if I'm needed at home, I can catch the next flight out. Tackle can finish things up for me here."

"Tackle?"

"Long story, sis. He's here in Italy."

"You're in Italy?"

"Yes...you're breaking up again. I'll be in touch when I land."

It was morning by the time I heard from Knox again. I called the office and told the lead on my team that I needed to pick my brother up at the airport. Given they all knew about the plane crash, no one questioned my taking the time off.

I thought about bringing him back to the apartment, but the idea of telling my brother I was pregnant in the same place it happened, turned my stomach.

Instead, I drove to a diner that was far enough from the city and far enough from Newton that I doubted we'd run into anyone we knew.

Thankfully, Knox didn't ask any questions until we were seated at a table in the back of the restaurant with no other customers in the vicinity.

"What's going on, Sloane?"

I bit my bottom lip, trying my hardest not to burst into tears. "I'm pregnant," I blurted.

My brother reached across the table and held his hands out to me. "I, um, don't know what to say, Sloane."

"I know. It's hard."

"Do the parents know?"

"No one knows, except the doctor and nurses I've seen."

"What about the father?"

"Not in the picture and never will be."

Knox nodded with scrunched eyes.

"Are you going to be able to handle that?" I asked, smiling for the first time, it seemed, since Friday.

My brother lowered his head momentarily, then looked back up at me. "Yes."

"Simple as that?"

Knox's eyes filled with tears, which he quickly tried to hide. "I told you at the airport, that day, that I want to be a better brother to you. I meant it. I can't tell you how good it makes me feel that I'm the person you reached out to for help."

"You understand I don't want anyone to know about this."

He smiled. "There will come a time they're gonna know, peanut." The look on his face changed. "I mean, if you're going to...you know."

"Have the baby?"

"Yeah."

"I have to, Knox."

"I get it, Sloane. I mean that. I hope you know I wasn't suggesting anything else."

I nodded. "I do."

"You're sure about the father not being in the picture?"

"One hundred percent." I turned my head away, feeling the onslaught of more tears.

"Look, it doesn't matter to me. I'm here. Whatever you need. I'm your guy."

I smiled through my tears. "Thanks, Knox."

"When do you plan to tell Mom and Dad?"

"I don't know yet."

"Fair enough."

"I have a question for you."

"Can I get you two something to eat?" said the waitress who'd finally approached our table.

"I haven't looked at the menu yet, have you?" Knox asked.

"You look. I know."

I ordered a double cheeseburger with fries, a salad, and a chocolate milkshake. "Don't say a word," I told Knox when he looked up at me with wide eyes.

"Same," he said to the waitress. "Except for the milkshake. I'll have coffee." Knox turned to me when she walked away. "You had a question?"

"How long will you be in town?"

"Indefinitely. Doc was in Italy too. I told him I was needed at home. He and Tackle said they'd cover me."

"Oh. I mean, that's nice."

"Tackle and I already talked about me working for his dad, so that's covered too."

"You *already* talked about it?"

"Before I left on this last job. He said there was plenty of work if I wanted it."

"By 'last job,' do you mean the missing-person case?"

"Yeah, but it got a whole helluva lot more complicated than that. Does the name Richard Emsworth mean anything to you?"

"Sounds familiar."

"It was his daughter, Tara, who was missing."

I raised a brow.

"Do you know her?"

I shook my head.

It took my brother twenty minutes to tell me what had transpired since he left at the beginning of January.

First, he'd tracked the daughter to Italy, where her father, who had been accused of art forgery as well as wire fraud, was purported to be.

Then after accusing *her* of being the forger, Knox had found out that the man he'd believed she was involved with but was actually her half brother, was responsible for the crimes. Something about the way he told the story told me he was leaving a lot out.

"Knox?" I asked between bites of my cheeseburger.

"Yeah?" he said, sitting back and wiping his mouth with his napkin.

"Did something happen between you and Tara Emsworth?"

He laughed. "Is it that obvious?"

16

Tackle

"Anything you wanna talk about?" Doc asked when he sat in the seat beside me shortly after we'd boarded the plane that would take us back to the States from Italy.

"Why, do I look like there is?"

"You have since Halo left."

"Did he say anything to you about what the emergency was?"

Doc shook his head. "I was going to ask you the same thing."

"Negative. I tried to call before we got in the air, but he didn't answer."

"You can try him again now."

"I left a message." I checked my phone, like I did at least every five minutes, but he hadn't responded. In fact, the only person I had heard from was the one person I'd hoped to never hear from again.

"Actually, Doc, there is something I'd like to talk to you about."

"Lay it on me, Landry."

"There's a woman...I, uh, went to high school with her. She turned up a few weeks ago, asking for my help. Abusive marriage."

"And?"

"I tried to get her to go to a shelter. She didn't want any part of that."

"What did you do instead?"

"My dad had a vacant rental property, so I put her up there. Called in a favor from Ranger Messick, who's been keeping an eye on her for me."

"I'm glad she came to you, Tackle. Sounds like there's more to it, though."

"She isn't the kind of person who likes being alone."

"And she wants you for company."

"You could say that."

"What do you know about the husband?"

"I think he's got connections."

"Hey, Sharp, got a sec?"

Razor got out of his seat, walked over, and sat down across from Doc and me. Razor was renowned for storing a computer-like database of criminals in his head. The man was uncanny.

"What's the husband's name?" Doc asked me.

"Dan Caruso. He lives in Waltham now, but I remember hearing he was from Providence."

Razor got up, grabbed his laptop, and came back. He sat with it closed, quiet for a few moments. "This guy about your age?" he asked.

"Affirmative."

"If I remember right, and I always remember right, someone by that name has known ties to Anthony 'Cadillac' DeLuca, the current head of the Sabatino family."

"Fuck," I muttered under my breath.

"When she came to you, was it because of a recent incident?" Doc asked.

"Yeah. He'd knocked her around the night before. Black eye, bruises on her arms and torso."

"Pattern of abuse?"

"Affirmative."

Razor opened his laptop. "Did she file a police report?"

"Negative. Said he had local law enforcement in his pocket."

"She was right about that," muttered Razor, who was typing something on his computer.

"You may not know this, but my first wife was in an abusive relationship before she and I got married," said Doc. "I'm going to caution you not to do what I did."

"Meaning?"

"Do not get involved with this woman for the wrong reasons."

"I'm trying hard not to get involved with her at all. She isn't making it easy, though."

"You did the right thing by trying to help her. Putting her up in your father's rental got her out of immediate danger, but it's time to move her somewhere else."

"Where?"

Doc got up. "Give me a few minutes to see what I can come up with."

"Tackle, you need to follow Doc's lead on this," said Razor. "The husband is bad news, not to mention he's practically in your backyard."

"Copy that."

A few minutes later, Doc returned to the seat next to me. "I was able to reach Ranger. I've also engaged Diesel Jacks to jump in on this. I've instructed them to move Ms. Caruso somewhere safe. However, according to Messick, the only way she'd agree to it is if he told her you would be meeting her at the new location."

"Where is the new location?"

"They should already be in California by the time we land."

"And then what?"

"I know I told you to remove yourself from the situation, but before you do, you need to convince her it's in her best interest to take the safe route we're offering."

"Roger that," I muttered, knowing I had to do what Doc was asking.

"What else, Tackle? Spit it out."

"I'm worried about whatever's going on with Halo's family."

Doc nodded. "I'll see what I can find out."

"He's downplaying whatever it is," Doc said after we'd landed in California and he was finally able to reach Halo. "I'll keep digging while you convince Ms. Caruso to go along with the plan we've made for her."

Doc asked Diesel to pick me up at the airfield and transport me to the house he'd arranged for Nick to stay in. While I waited, I called Halo myself.

"Hey, Tackle. You back from Italy yet?"

"Affirmative. Just landed in sunny California. How are things there?"

"Under control. For now, anyway."

"Anything I can do?"

"I don't think so."

"Let me know if that changes?"

"Will do. When will you be back?"

"I have a couple other things to take care of. Maybe another day or two."

"Copy that. Take care, man."

"You too." I ended the call, walked over to the airfield's bar, and ordered a shot, a beer, and another shot, knowing I'd need that and a whole lot more to get through the next couple of days with Nick.

17

Sloane

I heard my brother say Tackle's name when he answered his phone. As much as I wanted to ask about their conversation after the call ended, I couldn't without Knox getting suspicious.

"I've been thinking about you saying you don't really want to go back to Mom and Dad's right now, but how long can you realistically stay here?" he asked.

"Bex will be gone another three weeks at least. Maybe longer."

"Okay, well, that buys us some time to figure out what to do next." When Knox sat beside me on the sofa and put his arm around me, I rested my head on his shoulder.

"Thanks for all you're doing. I really appreciate it."

He laughed and kissed my forehead. "I haven't done much of anything yet, peanut."

"Just having you here is huge, but if you have to leave, I'll understand." I said the words but prayed he wouldn't have to.

"I'm not going anywhere. I told you that." He patted the sofa's cushion. "Except maybe to an apartment with more than one bedroom. I know you just said you could stay here another three weeks, but I'm thinking we start looking for another place tomorrow."

"You don't have to live with me, Knox."

"Sure, I do. It's not like I have anywhere else to live. We might as well share a place for the time being."

I yawned. "You're the best brother a girl could have."

"Making up for lost time, peanut. Now, get to bed."

I was so tired I didn't have the energy to argue that it was only seven o'clock.

As I lay in bed, staring up at the ceiling, unable to sleep when only minutes ago, I couldn't keep my eyes open, I thought about the story my brother had told me about his time in Italy.

"I fell in love with her, Sloane," he'd said. "I know it sounds crazy, but I did."

He talked more about how he'd gotten to know Tara while undercover at a winery in Tuscany. "Things were so good between us, and then I fucked it all up by accusing her of being a criminal."

I wanted to ask Knox how he could believe he loved her and yet get it that wrong, but I knew he was struggling with that question all on his own.

I also wanted to ask him a number of questions about when Tackle arrived in Italy, why he went, and what he was doing now that he was back. Instead, I rolled to my side and cried myself to sleep.

***

After spending over a week looking for a place for my brother and me to live, I sat Knox down and told him I didn't think it would work. He looked relieved.

"I have another idea, though."

I raised a brow, skeptical at his tone of voice.

"You know Tackle's dad owns a lot of investment property—"

"No!" I said before I could stop the word from flying out of my mouth.

Knox raised a brow like I had.

"They'll tell Mom and Dad."

"Hear me out."

I folded my arms, and Knox laughed. "You're so damn stubborn, peanut."

"Like you aren't," I mumbled.

"He's got a place halfway between home and your office. Literally less than eight miles from here."

"Where would you live?"

"A few blocks away, in one of their other rentals. It's a duplex, which would've been ideal, but the other side isn't inhabitable yet."

"I don't know..."

"You won't have to see his parents, or him, for that matter."

Tackle hadn't shown up unannounced since the day I ran out of the restaurant on him, so I doubted he would do that there.

"I don't want anyone to know I'm pregnant."

"There is no reason they'd have to. You're twenty-six years old, Sloane. It won't come as a surprise to anyone that you've decided to move out of our parents' house. I think it would raise more questions if you and I shared a place." He nudged me and laughed.

"I guess, but wouldn't it be just as easy for me to find a place that their family doesn't own?"

Knox shook his head. "It's a nice place in a safe part of town at a price that's unheard of. It will be impossible for you to find something similar."

"I don't want them to do me any favors."

Knox got up from the sofa and stalked over to the window. "Here are your choices. You live there, with the parents, or with me. Which one is it going to be?"

"Okay." After everything my brother had done for me, I couldn't argue with him.

Knox smiled. "Which one, peanut?"

"I'll live in Tackle's dad's place."

"I think it's the best option, or I wouldn't have suggested it."

"It's nice, right?" Knox said two hours later when he took me to see the rental.

Nice didn't begin to describe it. Even though it was a duplex, it felt more like a house. It had a front and back yard, and since the two units were separated by garages, it didn't feel any different than living in my parents' house had.

There were three bedrooms, including a master that was larger than any I'd ever seen. The kitchen was bright and sunny with a window that looked out at a tree with a swing hanging from one of its branches.

When Knox stood beside me and said, "Wouldn't be a bad place to raise a kid," I burst into tears.

He took a step back. "What just happened?"

I shrugged and grabbed a paper towel to blow my nose. "It's been happening with greater frequency."

Knox leaned against the kitchen counter. "Sloane, I know you don't want to talk about the baby's father, but I have to ask—"

"Don't."

"But—"

"I mean it, Knox. Don't go there."

"Will you let me speak if I promise not to ask a question?"

I folded my arms and glared at him. "I don't think it's possible."

He smiled. "If he knows and is leaving you on your own with this, he better hope I never know his identity. If he doesn't know, then I have to say, Sloane, you need to tell him."

I went out the back door, walked over to the swing, and after pulling on the ropes to make sure it was secure, sat on it. My brother followed.

"What if I told you I was inseminated?"

"I wouldn't believe you." He rubbed his arms. "Aren't you cold?"

I ignored his question about the temperature. "Why wouldn't you believe me?"

"You wouldn't have called me in Italy to ask me to come home."

I sighed. "You're right."

"Where are you guys?" I heard Tackle say from inside the house.

"What the fuck, Knox?"

He held up both hands. "I didn't even know he was back in town."

"Get rid of him."

"You don't have the words tattooed on your forehead. He isn't going to know you're—"

"*Shut up,*" I spat.

Knox walked in the direction of the house when Tackle came out the door. As I watched them embrace and pat each other's backs, I wondered if I was making the right decision about the baby. I'd have it; there was no doubt in my mind about that. It was my decision to keep him or her that I now questioned. Would their friendship be destroyed once the truth came out, as it inevitably would? I mean, Tackle could do the math.

Alternatively, with my brother's help, I could go away for a few months, give birth, find a family wanting to adopt, then come back and resume my life.

When my eyes met Tackle's, I knew I'd never be able to go through with that plan.

"Hey, peanut," he said, walking over to the swing. "Lift your feet and I'll push you."

"That isn't a good—"

"We aren't sure it's secure," I said, shooting daggers at my brother.

"I hear you're renting the place," Tackle said, following Knox and me back inside.

"I'm thinking about it."

He turned to Knox. "And you're renting half the duplex on Stanley?"

"That's right."

"I hope my dad gave you the family discount."

Knox did a funny thing with his head, and I watched as something passed between the two guys.

"What?" I asked.

"Nothing," Knox muttered before turning to Tackle. "Did you get everything taken care of?"

Tackle nodded, looked over at me, and back at my brother.

"This is ridiculous," I muttered, stalking toward the front door. "I'm going home." I got in my car and drove off. Since this place was so close to my parents' house, Tackle could give Knox a ride home.

18

Tackle

"What was that all about?" I asked.

"I wish I could tell you."

I turned my head and looked at Halo. He might as well have said, "I know, but I can't say."

"Is she okay?"

Rather than avoiding a straight answer, Knox didn't respond at all.

"What was the deal with the family-discount thing? Why'd you shake your head?"

"She doesn't know I'm paying half her rent along with mine."

"Why are you?" I had a pretty good idea what Sloane's salary was, and while this place wasn't cheap, she could afford the rent. At least more than half of it.

"I just am."

"You want a lift somewhere?" I asked when he locked the front door behind us.

"If you wouldn't mind."

Why would I mind? God, why did everything seem so off? Things were as fucked up between Knox and me as they were between Sloane and me.

Could I blame anyone other than myself for that? I was the one who'd started all this in motion the day I asked Sloane to meet me privately. I kept it going by having sex with her and turbocharged it by relentlessly pursuing her. And for what? More sex?

After spending two days convincing Nick that if she didn't take K19's relocation offer, I wouldn't be able to protect her, followed by another two days getting her settled in California, I had a clear picture of what a pain in the ass I'd been with Sloane.

Listening to Nick plead with me, even with different words than I'd used, sounded the same. The more she grated on my nerves, the more I regretted every single thing I'd said to Sloane. I'd fucking *stalked* her, for God's sake. No wonder she didn't want anything to do with me. Today, it seemed like she couldn't even stand being within five feet of me.

"Tackle?"

"What?" I snapped.

"Nothing." Halo took off on foot.

"Don't be an ass. Get back here. Of course, I'll give you a ride home."

"What's your problem, man?"

I rubbed my head, reminding myself I still hadn't gotten that haircut. "Nick."

"You with her now?" Halo asked.

"No." Furthest thing from it, actually, and I planned to keep it that way. "Her husband, he's, uh, bad news. Beat the crap outta her."

"Caruso?"

"Yeah. You know anything about him?"

"I've heard rumors."

"They were probably accurate."

"She still with him?"

I shook my head. "I made arrangements for her to live in one of my dad's rentals. On our way back from Italy, I confided in Doc about the situation and he stepped in."

"I'm guessing she's at an undisclosed location?"

"Affirmative."

"Shit. Think the husband knows you had anything to do with her 'disappearance'?" he asked after we were in the car on the way to his parents' place, where I hoped Sloane had gone too.

"I sure as hell hope not."

"I gotta ask, man. Why'd she come to you?"

I shrugged. "Nick always saw me as her way out of her lousy life. Her dad was an alcoholic, was violent toward her mother. I doubt she was ever as interested in me as she was in what I could do for her. When I was offered a full ride at UVA to play football, Nick got it into her head that someday I'd play for the NFL."

"I remember something about that. She started spreading rumors you might, even before we graduated."

"When she heard I was back in town, she assumed I was taking over my dad's business."

"She saw you as her meal ticket."

"And a way to get away from her husband."

"They say women go for men who are like their father. I guess she did with Caruso."

"Right."

"Who's funding this relocation? You?"

"Negative." It was something Doc and I had discussed before I left California.

"We plan to feed the feds enough for them to nab Caruso, who then might finger some more of DeLuca's crew."

"Keep driving," Halo said when I was getting close to his family's house.

"What's up?" I looked in the rearview.

"We have company."

"I know," I said, parking in front of the house. "He's with me."

Halo looked over his shoulder. "Who is that?"

"New guy. His name's Garrison Cassidy. Code name Cowboy."

"Get the fuck out."

"Totally serious."

"What's his cover?"

"Construction."

He smiled. "Guess I'll see him on the job site tomorrow."

"I'm glad we'll be working together, Halo."

When he didn't respond, I wondered if he thought I was lying.

A week later, I was cleaning up the project we'd been working on, when I heard Halo asking the other guys if they'd seen me.

"I'm over here," I shouted.

"Hey, I've got a favor to ask."

"Shoot."

"I'm having some furniture delivered to Sloane's place in about an hour. I could use some help."

My eyes met Cowboy's, who was standing behind Halo. "I wish you would've let me know earlier. I told my dad I'd meet him at another house he's looking to flip."

"No worries," he said, turning to walk away.

"Hey, Halo, I can help if you need it," Cowboy offered when I nodded.

"You sure?"

"Absolutely. I ain't got nothin' on except maybe havin' a couple of beers."

"I can make arrangements for that when we're done."

"Sorry, man," I called after them.

"It's all good," said Halo, waving behind him.

As much as I was dying to see Sloane, I couldn't yet. First, I had to be sure no one linked to Caruso had their sights set on me. There was no way I'd risk putting her in danger if Nick's husband knew I was the one who arranged for her to disappear.

Another two weeks had passed when I got a call from Razor.

"Just got word that Caruso's in custody."

"What for?"

"It's a long list, my friend. Racketeering, loan-sharking, tax fraud, stock manipulation, drug, and weapons possession."

"You've been busy."

"You know it. I also managed to plant the seed that he was looking to make a deal."

That was even better news. If anyone thought Caruso was ready to turn state's evidence, there was no way they'd help him with anything, including fingering me for getting his wife away from him.

"Thanks, Raze."

"No thanks necessary, Tackle. It's what we do."

I hung up, wishing I could celebrate by paying Sloane a visit. Instead, I went looking for Halo.

"Got time for a couple of Sammys after work?"

"Nothin' but time, man."

We went back to the grill and got there early enough that there weren't many people in the place.

"How's it goin'?" I asked after watching him pound his beer and throw back a shot of Irish.

"Okay, I guess."

"Tara?"

"She kicked me out of her life, Tackle. Not that I didn't deserve it. I fucked up pretty bad."

I'd heard the story from both him and Tara, and I had to admit I wasn't sure she'd ever come around. She might've forgiven him for lying about his identity, since she'd done the same thing, but his accusing her of being in the art-forgery business with her father, who had also turned out to be innocent, was something she couldn't get over.

"What do you think I should do?"

"Give her time," I responded, regretting it as soon as I did. What had I said to Sloane? I'd told her I couldn't be that guy anymore. I couldn't be passive, sitting around, waiting for something to happen that never would and then, after months had gone by, giving up completely. "Forget I said that."

Halo turned to me. "Said what? That I should give her time?"

"Yep. She'll never forgive you if she doesn't know how truly sorry you are."

"I apologized, Tackle. It wasn't enough."

"Make it enough."

"I wish I knew how."

When Halo ordered another round, I joined him, wondering why in the hell I wasn't following my own advice. My reasons for staying away from Sloane were twofold. First for her protection. Second, though, was me waiting until I thought enough time had passed that she might give me another chance. Another chance at what? What did I want from her? Until I knew the answer, I had no business asking for anything.

When Halo ordered his third shot, I agreed to join him only if he promised not to call Sloane to give our drunken asses a ride home.

"Poor peanut," he muttered. "She's got enough of her own shit to deal with."

"Is she okay?" All the weeks she'd been inexplicably sick raced through my mind. I hadn't talked to her since the doctor's appointment she'd told me she had scheduled. What if something was seriously wrong with her?

Halo threw the shot back. "Yeah. Sorry, Tackle. I shouldn't have said anything. I can't talk about it."

I put my arm on his and waited until he turned to look at me. "If she's ill, you have to tell me."

He hung his head. "She's not. Not in the way you're thinking." Halo took a swig of beer. "I've already said too much."

I suddenly regretted every ounce of alcohol I'd consumed. I wanted to get in my car and race over to Sloane's place and demand she tell me what was wrong. And I couldn't. Not shit-faced.

"Want another?" Halo asked, pointing at my beer.

"I think we've both had enough."

"What made you ask me to come out with you tonight?"

The bar had gotten significantly more crowded than it was when we arrived. "I'll tell you on our way out."

"Copy that."

"Where should we drop you?" Halo asked once we were in the cab.

"Same place you're going."

He rested his head against the back of the seat. "Sure, I guess you can crash there."

I laughed. "Thanks, man, but I meant next door. I'm going to be living there while I finish fixing it up."

He raised his head. "Seriously? That's awesome. We can hang out all the time. I can even help you with it."

"That would be great," I muttered, wishing I'd asked him to take me to my parents' place instead. How was I going to find time to see Sloane when I was with Halo twenty-four seven, either at work or at the duplex?

19

Sloane

Three months later

"But I miss you, *mija*," said my mother when I told her I didn't plan to come for Sunday dinner.

"I miss you too, but I can't come for dinner every week. I have my own place now."

"What about your laundry?"

"I have a washer and a dryer too." Thanks to Knox. In fact, my entire apartment was furnished thanks to my brother, who I had to admit had done a pretty good job of picking out things I liked.

He must've been paying attention when we toured all those apartments before we decided we shouldn't live together. The fun we'd had either laughing at or admiring the decorating tastes of whoever outfitted the furnished places, resulted in him knowing I would never want a flower-print sofa and, as far as I was concerned, sectionals should've gone the way of waterbeds years ago.

I had to admit I liked the deep-purple leather sofa and love seat along with the two blue leather recliners he'd picked out far more than I thought I would on the day they arrived. In fact, I'd asked him if the delivery people got the wrong address and if they were supposed to be for his place. Now, I couldn't imagine anything else in my living room.

He hadn't stopped there. I'd fallen in love with the other furniture he chose for the house too. At first, I told him he was crazy to fill up every room in my half of the duplex except one.

"We'll wait on the smaller bedroom," he'd said. "You'll want to pick stuff out based on the sex, right?"

"You know, bro, you're going to make a damn good husband to someone one day," I'd told him, only to realize that was the exact wrong thing to say when his face immediately sank.

"I think that boat has sailed, peanut."

"I'm sorry, Knox. I wish I had any advice, but I don't."

He'd left shortly after that, making me feel like the worst sister in the world.

***

A few days later, after convincing my mother that I wouldn't be coming over the next day, no matter how many of my favorite foods she promised to make, I went into the kitchen to make a batch of oatmeal raisin cookies.

When a knock at the door startled me, I dropped the glass bowl I'd taken out of the cupboard. Thankfully, it was heavy enough that it didn't break, although it looked like there were a couple of chips along the edge.

"Hey, Sloane? It's me," I heard Tackle say, knocking a second time.

I set the bowl on the counter, glanced at the mirror to make sure my oversized sweatshirt hid the baby bump that had recently appeared but seemed to be growing daily, and slowly walked toward the front entrance. I looked around the living room to see if there were pregnancy or baby books visible. When I didn't see any, I opened the door.

"What are you doing here?"

"I wanted to come by and see if you needed anything."

"Nope. I'm good." I stood in the doorway, letting him know I had no intention of inviting him in.

"Sloane, I haven't seen you in weeks. Can I please come in?"

Those damn green eyes did me in every time. "For a few minutes," I said after stepping aside.

"What did I interrupt?" he asked, eyeing the things I'd gotten out to make the cookies.

"Girl's night in."

"Oh. Is someone else here?"

"No. Just me. I meant I was staying in. Cookies and a movie."

"How are you feeling?" he asked with an overly concerned edge to his voice.

"Fine. Why?"

"I haven't talked to you in so long. Did you figure out what was wrong over the holidays?"

"It was nothing," I said, putting the butter in the microwave to soften.

"I'm glad." He looked around. "I like what you've done to the place."

"Most of it was Knox's doing, but thanks. I never expected to like living on my own as much as I do."

"You don't get lonely?"

"Not really, and if I did, my mother would be more than happy to keep me entertained."

He laughed, but then his expression changed. I followed his line of sight to where today's mail sat on the counter. There, right on top, sat the *Mama & Baby* magazine I'd recently subscribed to. Before I could get to it, Tackle picked it up and turned it over, most likely to confirm I was the subscriber.

When he set it back down, I hated the way his eyes trailed down my body.

"You need to leave."

He made no move to. In fact, he pulled a chair away from the dining room table, turned it around, and sat down so he was facing me. "Is there something you need to tell me?"

"No," I said, turning my back to him. I closed my eyes and took a deep breath. I'd spent endless hours concocting the story I'd tell Tackle when the day came he found out I was pregnant. With him sitting a few feet from me, I couldn't remember any of it.

"Sloane," he whispered, walking over and resting his hands on my shoulders. "Don't make me ask again."

"It isn't yours," I said as tears streamed down my cheeks.

"Tell me the truth," he said without raising his voice. Before I could respond, he spun me around and pulled me into his arms. "Why didn't you tell me?"

"You don't want kids," I said so softly I wasn't sure he could even hear me.

He pulled back and looked into my tear-filled eyes. "This is why you called Knox in Italy and asked him to come home." He cradled my head, still looking into my eyes. "He doesn't know I'm the father."

"No."

Tackle took a step back and pulled me with him over to the sofa. He cuddled me close to him when we both sat.

"I want you to know I don't expect—"

"Shh." He put his fingertip on my lips. "Give me a minute. Okay?" Those damn green eyes stared into mine, imploring again.

"Okay."

"Your brother went to New York City to see Tara."

"I know."

"That's why I came over."

"I figured that's why."

"Do your parents know?"

I shook my head. "I can't keep it from them much longer."

Tackle grasped my chin with his hand and brought his lips to mine. He kissed me, gently at first, then demanding, then gently again. "Every minute of every day since I last saw you, I've thought about how much I wanted to kiss you."

I shook free of his grasp and turned my head away from him.

"I need to tell you something, and for me to do that, I need you to look at me."

"No," I cried.

"Sloane, please." He slid off the sofa and knelt in front of me. "Please," he repeated. "I want this baby. I want you. I need you to tell me you understand what I'm saying."

I looked into his eyes. "I don't."

"Tomorrow, we'll tell your parents and mine. We'll go to them together. Tell them we're getting married—"

"Have you lost your mind?" I shrieked, wrenching away from him. I stood and stalked into the kitchen. "*No! God!* I'm not marrying you, Tackle."

"But—"

When he stood in front of me, I shoved him away. "Get out! Just leave."

He came right back and put his hands on my shoulders. "I'm not leaving. We have a lot to talk about."

"You're wrong. We have nothing to talk about." I stalked down the hall and into the bedroom, closing the door and locking it behind me. It wouldn't make him leave, but he also wouldn't break the door down.

I lay on the bed and waited, knowing that at any second, he'd beg me to let him in, telling me we needed to talk. Instead, I heard the front door close. After a few minutes of silence, I crept from the bedroom and out to the living room. It was empty. I walked over, threw the deadbolt, turned off the lights, and peered out the window. Sure enough, his car was no longer in the driveway. Racing into the kitchen, I grabbed my phone when something occurred to me.

Punching in his name, I hurriedly unblocked his number and called him.

"You better not be on your way to my parents' house," I said when I heard him answer.

"Wow," he muttered. "After all this time hiding the fact that you were pregnant, refusing to see me or talk to me, blocking my number, *that's* what you wanted to say?"

"It isn't your place to tell them. I'll tell—"

"I would never do that, Sloane."

20

Tackle

I ended the call, tossed the phone on the passenger seat, pulled off on a side street, parked, and rested my head on the steering wheel.

Thoughts raced through my head faster than I could process them. That's what she thought of me? That when she refused to marry me, I'd rush over to her parents' house and tell them to force her to?

Why didn't she *want* to marry me? She was pregnant with *my* baby. Why the fuck hadn't she told me? Why had she kept it from me? Was I really that bad of a guy? What had I ever done to make her think I was?

Clearly, Halo didn't know the baby was mine. If he did, he wouldn't have been able to hide the fact he knew. More, he probably would've beat the shit out of me long before this.

Who in the hell had she told him the father was? How had my friendship with him reached the point where he didn't think he could confide in me about this?

"Poor peanut," he'd said. "She's got enough of her own shit to deal with."

I counted back the number of weeks since he'd returned from Italy. Everything that had happened made so much more sense now.

That was the emergency. Sloane was pregnant. He'd arranged for a place for her to live, underwrote her rent, because she was pregnant. He'd even hesitated going to New York this weekend, almost passed up the chance to see Tara, because Sloane was pregnant.

I counted again. This time, the number of weeks between the first time she and I had had sex, when the condom broke, and when she had the mysterious illness.

I didn't know a damn thing about how women felt when they were pregnant; maybe Sloane didn't either. I knew she never got the message about the broken condom because it showed up on my phone as not being delivered.

I put the car back in gear. Instead of going to the duplex, I drove home—to my parents' house.

"Everything okay?" my mother asked when I walked in the door that led from the garage into the kitchen.

"I need to talk to you, Mom."

She set down the dish towel she had in her hand. "Okay."

"Where's Dad?"

"Watching a movie. What's going on, Landry?"

"Can we go for a drive?"

"Of course. Let me grab my coat."

"What will you tell him?"

"Your father?"

I nodded.

"I'll come up with something." My mom, bless her heart, winked at me before walking away. She was back in not much longer than it would've taken for her to get the coat she hadn't yet put on. She held it out for me to help her with it. "I told him we were going for ice cream."

"In the dead of winter?"

"Why not? We used to go for ice cream all the time. The weather didn't matter."

Once she buttoned her coat, I hugged her. "Thanks, Mom."

"Come on, let's get out of here before he decides to come with us."

"I'm guessing this has something to do with Sloane," she said after I'd backed my car out of the garage and the door had closed.

I put my foot on the brake. "What makes you say that?"

"The two of you have tiptoed around each other long enough. For goodness' sake, why don't you admit what everyone else already knows?"

"Who knows what already?"

"The two of you are crazy about each other."

I backed the rest of the way out of the driveway and drove a mile down the road to the town park.

"Why are you stopping here?" my mother asked when I pulled up to the curb.

"What do you mean?"

"I thought we were going to get ice cream."

"I thought that's just what you told Dad. Do you really want to?"

"Of course I do."

"Okay, but wait. Before we do that, there's something I need to tell you."

"Go ahead."

"Sloane's pregnant."

"I see." My mother turned in her seat so she was facing me. "Your baby, I take it?"

I raised a brow, and she put her hand on mine. "How far along is she?"

"I don't know." I counted on my fingers. "Five months?"

"And you found out tonight?"

I nodded. "She didn't tell me."

"That's why Halo's been in Newton," she mumbled.

"I don't know how you figured that out, but yeah."

She nodded and turned so she was facing forward again. "Let's go. This calls for a sundae. Maybe even a banana split."

"Mom, I need you to take this seriously."

She looked back at me. "Make no mistake. I'm taking this very seriously, Landry."

"Okay, but we can't talk about it while we're in there."

"You don't say."

"When did they add a drive-thru?" I asked while we waited for our order.

"I think you were fourteen or fifteen."

"Seriously?"

She laughed. "I can't tell you how many times I wondered how you got a job with the CIA."

"Very funny."

"So how did you leave things with her?"

"Pretty much the same as always. I said the wrong thing, and she's no longer speaking to me."

"Oh dear. What did you say?"

"I told her I'd be with her when she told her parents and she'd be with me when I told you and Dad."

"That's it?"

"Not exactly."

"What else?"

"I said we'd tell you both we were getting married."

"Hang on. You're getting married?" she gasped.

"Why is that a surprise? She's pregnant."

"Landry, do your best to try to remember your exact words."

"Those were my exact words."

"No. Tell me how you asked her to marry you."

When I turned my head and looked out the window instead of at her, my mother swatted my arm.

"You didn't, did you?"

"She's pregnant."

"Good Lord, Landry. No wonder she isn't speaking to you."

"So what do I do?"

She motioned in front of the car. "Pull forward."

"About Sloane?"

"I knew what you meant. I'm thinking."

I opened the window and took our order from the hands of a girl who looked really familiar.

"Hey, it's you," she said. "Remember me? From the pizza place?" The girl bent down and looked into the car. "Is that your mom?"

I groaned, rolled up the window, and drove away.

"I can tell you what not to do. Under no circumstances should you bring Sloane here for ice cream."

I drove back to the park, and we sat in silence, eating our ice cream. My mom looked lost in thought, which I hoped meant she was preparing to tell me what to do.

Finally, she spoke. "Let me ask you this. Do you love Sloane?"

Of all the things she could've asked, that was the hardest for me to answer. I mean, of course I loved her, but was I in love with her? In love enough to marry her?

"Before you make Sloane any other offers—or in your case, demands—decide how you feel about her."

I glared at her over the demand comment. "I meant well, Mom."

"Beside the point, Landry. You bulldozed over Sloane's feelings. You are aware she has feelings, right?"

"Do you not understand how hard this is for me?"

Apparently, that was the absolute wrong thing for me to say, given the look she gave me was the same as ones I'd seen from Sloane.

She took a deep breath and let it out slowly. "I'm glad you said that, because it's exactly what you need to think about, Landry. How hard is this on you versus how hard it is on Sloane. She's five-months pregnant, and until tonight, it sounds as though the only person she's been able to lean on is Knox."

"Right."

"What are you prepared to offer her? What kind of life, Landry? Do you plan to take over your father's construction business one day? Is that how you'll support your family? Or are you planning to continue working in intelligence?"

I started to answer, but she held up her hand. "Where do you plan to live? And the most important question of all is, if you don't love her, why would you think she would agree to marry you?"

As I listened to my mother's questions, I thought about the many I'd asked myself when I left Sloane's place. It hadn't occurred to me until now how much I was like her, at least in the way we processed through our thoughts and emotions.

"Landry?"

"Yeah, Mom?"

"How do you feel about having a child?"

"You gotta ask the hard questions, don't you?"

My mother laughed and shrugged. "Do you have an answer?"

"It's changed from what I would've said yesterday."

"Tell me yesterday's answer first."

"No way in hell would I want a kid at this point in my life."

"And now?"

I turned in my seat and looked into my mother's eyes. "It's Sloane, Mom. Can you imagine what an amazing mother she'll be, not to mention how awesome the kid will be?"

Her eyes filled with tears. "Just as awesome as you are, Landry. It's exactly how your father and I felt when I found out I was pregnant."

"I couldn't imagine wanting to have a baby with anyone else."

"And yet, you aren't certain if you love her."

21

Sloane

I paced the kitchen, changing my mind as often as I changed direction. Maybe I'd been wrong to call him, assuming he'd go to my parents. As he said, he'd never do that. I *knew* he wouldn't.

Instead of wearing a hole in the kitchen floor, I decided to clean up the mess I'd made earlier. I should've finished making the cookies. At least then I'd have something to binge on besides sappy rom-coms that only made me cry.

I opened the lower cupboard to put my chipped bowl away when someone pounded on my front door. For the second time, I dropped the damn thing. "*What?*" I shouted out.

"Sloane, it's me, Tackle."

"Argh," I grumbled, walking over to the door that I flung open. "What?" I repeated, only slightly less angrily.

"I want a do-over."

I leaned against the door and sighed. "What do you mean?"

"Let's do the whole thing over. Everything that happened earlier tonight."

"That isn't possible."

"Sure, it is." He cleared his throat. "Uh, Sloane, I haven't seen you in weeks. Can I please come in?"

I took a step back and waved him in, knowing damn well I couldn't deny him and his puppy-dog eyes.

He walked over and picked up the magazine. "I wish I could come up with something different to say about this." He set it back down. "I'll skip ahead a little."

When he held his hand out, I took it. He pulled me over to the sofa, and when I sat down, he knelt in front of me.

"May I?"

"What?"

He reached under my sweatshirt, rested his hand on my belly, and looked up at me. "Wow."

That alone was almost enough for me to forgive him anything and everything. I put my hand on top of his. "Do you feel that?"

He shook his head, but otherwise, we both remained perfectly still.

"What about that?"

"No." His eyes opened wide. "Wait. Was that something?"

I shrugged. "It just started happening, so I'm not sure. Could be a muscle twitch."

Tackle reached up with his free hand and grasped my neck, pulling me closer until our lips met. When he kissed me, I put both my arms around him, and he did the same.

"Sloane?"

"Shh." I put my fingertip on his lips. "Give me a minute, okay?"

He smiled. "I'll give you all the time you need, peanut."

"You seem happier than earlier."

He cupped my cheek with his palm. "There's something I need to tell you."

"Okay."

"Before I do, please know that she will not tell a soul, including my father."

"You told your *mother*?" I tried to wriggle away from him, but this time, he held me tight where I was.

"Sloane, I swear to you that she will not tell anyone."

I felt dizzy and closed my eyes. "If she—"

"She won't. I promise you."

"Is that what you had to tell me?"

He sat on the sofa, next to me. "No."

I leaned my head against the cool leather. "There's more?"

"You said I seem happier."

"I'm struggling with caring about your happiness, Tackle. I can't believe you told your mother."

He rested his head on the back of the sofa like I had. "I *really* need to tell you this."

I sighed. "Okay. Go ahead."

"My mom asked me how I felt about having a baby. I told her that if she'd asked me that yesterday, I would've said no way in hell I wanted one at this point in my life."

Every muscle in my body tightened, almost like rigor mortis.

"And then I told her today's answer." Tackle put his fingers on my chin and turned my face toward him. "Which was—and I'm going verbatim here—'It's Sloane, Mom. Can you imagine what an amazing mother she'll be, not to mention how awesome the kid will be?'"

"Did you really say that?" I asked, trying my damnedest not to cry.

"I really did. Word for word."

"What does she think?"

"That I handled things with you like a total jackass."

"What does she think about me?"

"That if you're smart, like she knows you are, you'll kick me to the curb. She's also praying you'll give me another chance." His eyes bored into mine. "Will you?"

"It isn't that simple. There's still the matter of my brother, who will likely kill you when he finds out."

"Kill me? I figured he'd throw a couple of punches. You really think he'll kill me?"

"You're not funny. He's going to be really mad, Tackle, and you know it. My parents will be too. At least my mom will be. She'll be mad at both of us."

"I'm not so sure."

"You're wrong if you're not sure."

"My mom seems to think that the two of us have been—how did she put it— 'tiptoeing around each other long enough, and why won't we admit what everyone else already knows.'"

"Get the fuck out."

"She really said it."

"Not Knox. He isn't part of *everyone.*"

"No. He's not. This will blindside him."

I could feel Tackle's sadness about my brother's reaction as much as I could feel my own.

"He'll think we betrayed him."

Tackle pulled me close and kissed the side of my face. "I don't know about that. He'll be angry and probably hurt, but at the end of the day, he loves both of us."

"That's true."

"I'm sorry about the whole 'getting married' thing. I seriously blew that one too."

I started to giggle, and once I had, I couldn't stop. Pretty soon, Tackle was laughing too.

"It was so Neanderthally."

"You'd love what my mom said about that."

"Did you tell her everything?"

"About our conversation? Yeah. She kind of pulled it out of me. She said it wasn't a surprise that you weren't speaking to me."

I put my hand over my mouth to stifle my yawn.

"You're tired. I should go."

What I was about to do was probably monumentally stupid, but I couldn't stop myself. "Stay." I'd rarely seen Tackle speechless, but he was now. "Please stay."

"You really want me to?"

"A lot."

He laughed and then got serious. "What about Halo?"

I picked up my phone that sat on the coffee table. I held it up for him to read my brother's text.

Staying in the city. Didn't want you to worry.

"That's a good sign. For him, I mean."

"I thought so too. Also good for us."

"You really want me to stay?"

"Oh my God. Yes. How many times do I have to say it?" Perhaps equally stupid was the next thing I did, and that was to stand and remove every stitch of my clothing.

22

Tackle

"You look so fucking beautiful," I said when Sloane stood before me naked. "Come closer." I motioned with my finger.

I realized as I took my time studying the changes in her body that, sometime in the last few years, she'd become the woman I measured all others by, without my even noticing it.

Her body was the sexiest I'd ever seen. Her boobs were fuller than when I'd last held their weight in my hands, and her tummy was rounder. Overall, she had more meat on her bones.

I thought about the weeks since I'd seen her naked. There was a reason Sloane had walked out on me that day when I sat in the restaurant across the street from her friend's apartment. She'd been right in her assessment of what I was saying even before I finished speaking. I was pushing her away, letting her know that while I liked her, I wasn't interested in a relationship. I realized now what utter bullshit that had been.

When I saw chill bumps on her skin, I led her into the bedroom and pulled the comforter and sheet back.

"Under the covers, Sloane."

She watched with wide eyes while I removed my clothes and got into bed next to her. I pulled her close so her head rested in the crook between my shoulder and chest.

"Tackle?"

"Peanut?"

"Is there something wrong?"

"I don't think so. Why do you ask?"

"You aren't…you know."

I shifted so I was facing her and plumped the pillow under her head. "There's nothing wrong."

"Then, why aren't you touching me?"

I smiled when she put my hand on her breast.

"If I recall correctly, it wasn't that long ago you referred to me as a Neanderthal."

Sloane put her hand on top of mine and squeezed. "That was your brain, not your body."

I couldn't help myself; I laughed. "There are so many things I like about you, Sloane."

"I could say the same about you."

"But you won't?"

The playfulness was gone from her expression. "I don't want you to be with me just because of the baby."

I caressed her cheek with the tip of one finger. "I'm sorry I made you think that was the case."

"Tackle, I…um…"

"Whatever you're struggling to say, just say it."

"I want this baby."

I had no idea what point she was trying to make, since I wouldn't have expected anything else.

"But I don't want you to feel like you have to make any commitments right now."

Rather than respond, I scooted down the bed. I put my hands on either side of her belly, leaned forward, and kissed the slight protrusion. "Hey, little peanut, put in a good word with your mom for me, okay?"

Sloane rested her hand on one of mine.

I stayed where I was but looked up at her. "I want to be a part of both your lives. A big, permanent part. I understand, though, why you'd question my level of commitment or even why you think I'm only here because of this little one." I splayed the fingers of my hand. "But it's more than that, Sloane."

She nodded, but her look remained skeptical. "There's something I need to ask you."

"Anything."

Sloane smirked. "I can ask, right? That doesn't mean you can answer."

"Your security clearance is probably higher than mine."

"About that. I've requested to be moved to a different division."

I felt my shoulders tense. "Where?"

"Still here. And by here, I mean working from home."

"Doing what?"

"Cyber. Data analysis primarily. It isn't much different than what I do now, except I won't have any fieldwork."

"I like the sound of that." I kissed her belly again. "She's already such a good mom to you."

"What about you, Tackle?"

"I have a job with my dad. Eventually, the business will be mine." She didn't look happy. "What?"

"And be miserable." She rolled away and sat up. "I'm pregnant, so you not only give up your bachelor lifestyle, but you work a job you never intended to be a career. Don't do this, Tackle." Sloane grabbed a robe and walked out of the room. I followed—without a robe.

"You can switch careers, but I can't?"

"I'm not switching careers; I'm changing divisions." Her eyes trailed down my naked body, immediately bringing my cock back to full attention. I had to focus on our conversation, though, not on how much I desperately wanted her.

"And yet, if I said I was going to take a permanent job with K19, you'd kick me to the curb even faster." I sounded irritated because I was.

"Is that what you want to do?"

"Does any of this really need to be decided tonight?"

"You're the one who wanted to talk."

My eyes scrunched. "I did?"

"You didn't want to do anything else."

"There's a difference between not wanting to and trying to do the right thing."

"Stop trying to do the right thing, Tackle."

"What about the baby?"

Sloane walked over to the sofa's end table and opened the drawer. She pulled out a book and flipped to a page that had been dog-eared. "According to this, it's perfectly okay to have sex while pregnant." She thrust it at me, but I didn't take it.

"I trust your word," I said with a wink.

"Is it because you don't find me attractive anymore?"

"I'm not sure what would make you say that, but"—I made a sweeping motion across the lower half of my body—"clearly, that is not the case." Her brow was furrowed, and I swear her lower lip was protruding. I held out my hand and, when she took it, led her back to the bedroom.

I moved the covers for the second time and motioned for her to lie down.

"I don't want to do anything to hurt you or the baby. That was the only reason I hesitated."

I waited for her to say something, but all she did was turn her back to me.

"Sloane? What's going on?"

"What happened to 'When we're together like this, naked, whatever I tell you to do, you do'?"

"Ah, I see." I put my arm around her waist and pulled her body flush with mine. "Did you like that, Sloane?"

She nodded.

"I need to hear the words." I rubbed the cheeks of her bare bottom in warning.

"I liked it."

"Liked what?"

"When you told me what to do."

I closed my eyes and breathed in the scent of her. Was there a more perfect woman for me? I doubted one could possibly exist.

"Roll over and face me, Sloane." When she did without hesitation, my already steel-hard cock throbbed with desire. "I've missed you so much."

"I've missed you too."

"Have you?"

She nodded.

"You kept me away for so long."

Her eyes studied mine.

"Don't ever do that again."

She didn't respond.

"Promise me."

When she remained silent, I swatted her bottom.

"Promise me, Sloane."

Her eyes filled with tears, but not from my hand on her flesh; I'd barely tapped her.

"Tell me what you're thinking, peanut."

"I can't make that promise," she whispered.

"Why not?"

She shook her head.

"Because you don't trust me."

She didn't need to answer; I hadn't phrased it as a question.

"Let's sleep."

"You're angry."

"Not at all. You were honest with me, and that is another rule I insisted on between us."

"But you don't want to have sex?"

"There are so many things we need to talk through, figure out, decide about. I don't want to confuse the issues with sex. That's different than not wanting to."

23

Sloane

While I'd never admit it now, I knew Tackle was right. We'd gone from pseudo-friends to lovers with little communication between us. Perhaps if we'd talked more things through, I wouldn't have spent the last three months in turmoil over what to do about the baby. Instead of having my brother with me for my doctor's appointments, the father could have been there. The idea that I'd denied him that opportunity made me sad.

The first time I heard the baby's heartbeat, I cried. When I saw his or her shape on the screen as the tech pressed the cold, hard ultrasound wand against my abdomen, I cried too. In fact, I'd cried more in the last three months than I had at any other time of my life, except for maybe when I was an infant.

Knox had comforted me, of course, but even then, I regretted Tackle not being with me.

I cupped his cheek like he'd done so many times with me. "I'm sorry."

"What for?"

"I'll tell you tomorrow."

Tackle laughed and pulled me closer to him, if that was possible. If only we could be like this all the time, it would be heaven for me. I'd loved him for so long, never believing there was a chance he'd ever love me.

I still doubted it was possible. I even questioned whether he really, *truly* wanted our baby. How did someone go from "no way in hell do I want one at this point in my life" to "promise me you'll never keep me away" in the span of a couple of hours?

Based on my own experience, he'd change his mind daily, if not more often, about how he felt about being a parent.

There were times I thought it was the greatest blessing I could've been given. Others, I wondered what in the world I thought I was doing. Now that Tackle knew, maybe I could tell my mom like he'd told his. Being able to talk to her, and to my dad, about it, would be such a relief. Knox, however, was an entirely different matter.

He'd been so patient with me, putting me first above all else, being there whenever I needed him. How could he not feel betrayed by the fact that I hadn't told him the father was his own best friend?

"You're not sleeping," he murmured.

"Neither are you."

"There's an appendage between my legs that is in complete disagreement about sleep being necessary."

"There's something between my legs that agrees with your appendage."

"If we make them both happy, maybe they'll let us sleep."

I wanted him so much that if I were standing, I'd hurl my body at his.

When I felt Tackle's fingers between my legs, all thought stopped. I only allowed myself to feel. I'd craved this.

"Sloane?" he whispered.

I looked into his eyes.

"I don't want to use a condom, but I have to know you're okay with that."

"I trust you, Tackle."

When I felt his skin against mine as his hardness went deeper and deeper into me, I lost track of everything but pleasure. I writhed, I groaned, I pleaded, and I orgasmed. Again and again throughout the night.

"This is a dream come true," said Tackle when he woke and my hand was on his penis.

"I thought maybe I'd worn you out."

"If I had more energy, you'd get a swat for saying that."

"How did you know you, ya know, liked that?"

"Swatting your perfect ass?" He gave me two slaps to prove his point, I suppose.

"Ouch and yes."

"Instinct. The same way you know it excites you when I put my hands on your breasts or my fingers in your hot, wet pussy. Speaking of which..." He stroked through my folds and pushed inside me.

"Did the other, uh, other people you've been with, like it too?"

"Are you sure you want to talk about this?"

"I absolutely don't, but it'll drive me crazy until we do."

"Some liked it. Some didn't."

"I see."

"I warned you." He squeezed one of my cheeks and pressed his fingers deeper. "Now, you tell me, do *you* like it, Sloane?"

"You know I do," I groaned when he curled his fingers and touched that elusive spot I hadn't believed existed.

"Good thing you didn't try to lie."

“Oh my God,” I cried when he brought his mouth to my pussy and licked me.

We spent another hour in bed, and when Tackle got up, I knew he’d be leaving soon. I checked my phone for a message from my brother, but there weren’t any. Who knew when he might be back in Boston? We couldn’t risk him driving by and seeing Tackle’s car in the driveway.

“We need to tell him,” said Tackle after he’d gotten dressed. “I don’t want to hide.”

“I don’t either.” I hadn’t been hiding from Knox, at least not completely. It was Tackle and everyone else that I’d kept as far away from as possible, and it was exhausting.

“Do you think I should tell my parents first or my brother?”

He sat back down on the bed. “I think *we* should tell them.”

“You told your mom on your own.”

“Only because I was worried I’d fucked things up with you forever.” He leaned over and kissed me. “I’ll call you in a couple of hours, and we’ll figure out our day.”

Figure out our day? What did that mean?

Tackle laughed. "You are so transparent."

"What do you mean?"

"I totally just freaked you out." I could hear him laughing all the way out the front door.

He hadn't been gone more than twenty minutes when my cell phone rang with a call from my brother.

"Hey, peanut," he said when I answered.

"Hi. Where are you?"

"Still in New York City."

"Does that mean it went well with Tara?"

"I told her I loved her."

"And?"

"She said it back."

I wiped at the tears already running down my cheeks. "Oh, Knox. I'm so happy for you."

"Listen, Sloane, I want to stay down here a couple more days."

"Do it."

"Are you going to be okay on your own?"

"I will be. I promise."

"Will you call me if you're the least bit uncomfortable?"

I laughed. "And what? You'll come rub my feet?"

"If that's what you need."

"Tell you what, rub Tara's feet instead."

"I can't wait for you to meet her."

I heard another voice in the background. "You better go. Just keep me posted on when you think you'll be coming back."

"I need to check in with work and see if I can get Monday off."

I laughed. "Do you really think Tackle would make you come back?"

"You know something I don't, peanut? Did Tackle get a promotion in the last twenty-four hours? The last I checked, his dad still ran the company."

"I didn't mean anything by it, Knox."

"Right. Okay, gotta go. Again, if you need me, I'm a little over an hour away."

Less than an hour later, Tackle showed back up at my place.

"Did you talk to my brother?" I asked when I opened the door.

He answered by walking over the threshold and wrapping me up in his arms. "He won't be back until Wednesday at the earliest."

"Oh." I hadn't expected he'd be gone five days. I hadn't been away from my brother for that long since February.

"You okay?"

"Of course."

"There's something I want to show you."

"Where are we going?" I asked when Tackle drove down one of the area's most historic streets.

"A house I want to show you."

"In this neighborhood?"

Tackle reached over and took my hand. "Keep an open mind."

"Houses in Chestnut Hill go for millions of dollars."

He laughed. "Not all of them." He slowed the car. "Close your eyes."

"No."

"Pretend you're naked, Sloane."

"What?"

"Just do it."

"Oh my God. Okay, I'm naked."

"Now, close your eyes."

As much as it had been a joke a few seconds ago, when Tackle used his growly, gravelly voice, his wish was my command.

The car kept moving, but slowly, then stopped. "Eyes still closed?"

"Yes."

"Do not open them."

"Yes, sir," I joked.

His door closed, and seconds later, mine opened.

"Closed," he whispered as something soft covered my eyes. Whatever it was, felt like silk, and he tied it at the back of my head. "Give me your hand."

Tackle helped me from the car and, with one arm around my back and the other holding my hand, led me a few feet from it. "We'll be going up ten steps. Ready?"

I nodded.

"A few feet more."

"I don't like this."

"Trust me, Sloane."

We stopped, and he removed the silk covering my eyes. "Okay, open."

I gasped. "You remembered," I said so quietly I almost couldn't hear myself speak.

"When my dad asked me to meet him here a few weeks ago, I couldn't believe it."

Back when our family first moved to Newton, Tackle and my brother used to come to the park on the other side of the street and play football. It was where Knox broke his neck.

One day, they brought me with them; I couldn't remember why. My parents had probably asked my brother to babysit.

Instead of watching whatever they were doing, I sat on a bench and stared across the street at the house I now stood under the portico of.

It was dilapidated then, and now it was worse, but when I looked at it, all I could see was its former grandeur.

I turned around to look at the park and wondered why Tackle had brought me here. "Is it for sale?"

He shook his head. "Not anymore."

"Oh."

"Come on, let's go in."

"We can't."

"Sure, we can." He kept a tight grasp on my hand with one of his while he opened the front door with the other.

"They just left it open?"

"Not quite." He closed the door behind us. "How about a tour?"

"Tackle—"

He pulled me into his arms and kissed me. "Trust me," he repeated.

"Okay."

We walked into the foyer. On the left was a formal dining room, and on the right, a parlor. Both had big windows that looked out over the expanse of the front lawn and the park across the street.

"There used to be a piano that sat in this front window," I said, surprising myself at the memory.

"This is one of four fireplaces," Tackle said, pointing to it as we walked out of that room, down the hallway to the door that led to the kitchen.

It was twice as large as my parents', and while I'd never considered a kitchen beautiful, this one was. It had high ceilings and more cupboards than I'd ever seen in a person's home. "Is someone renovating the place?" I asked, running my hand over the brand-new chef's cooktop.

"Someone is." Tackle went back through the swinging door. "This is where the second fireplace is," he said, motioning to a sitting room smaller than the front parlor. Windows with a view of the backyard lined two of the outer walls. "The house sits on two acres—almost unheard of in this part of the state."

He led me over to the staircase; I followed him up and to the front of the house.

"This is the master bedroom. The bathrooms need more work than other parts of the house, other than the kitchen."

There was a window seat that stretched out across three-quarters of the room. I remembered that too and the daydreams I'd had about sitting on it and reading. I couldn't help but wonder why Tackle was talking about the place so intimately. "Is this one of your dad's projects?" I asked.

"Sort of." He walked through another doorway. "There is plenty of room for a large bathroom as well as a walk-in closet. Two, actually."

Still at the front of the house but across the hall sat another small bedroom.

"There's one more bedroom on this floor, and behind the master is what once might have been that era's laundry room."

"You're kidding." I went down the hall and through the swinging door. The room's floor and backsplash were white tile, and it had cupboards similar to those in the kitchen.

Tackle pointed to a back staircase. "Your favorite method of escape," he said, winking. "The third floor has four small bedrooms and what was probably once a sitting area. My guess is two of the rooms were for the servants and the other two were part of a nursery."

"It's amazing, Tackle. Thank you for bringing me here. I've always wanted to see what it looked like inside. I can't wait to see what whoever owns it will do with it."

He walked closer to where I stood and took both my hands in his. "Sloane, I own it."

"What?" I gasped.

"My father and I, but with the idea that once I'm able to buy him out, I will."

I leaned against the wall. "Why?"

"My mother said it was a premonition."

I closed my eyes when the vertigo I'd experienced last night returned. "I don't understand."

"I'm renovating it, Sloane, with my father's help. My intention is to make it a home."

"For whom?"

"I won't make the same mistake I did last time with assumptions, but I hope one day you'll consider living here with me."

I put my hand on my belly when I thought I felt the baby move.

"Do you want to see the rest of it?"

I still felt too dizzy to walk. "There's more?"

"We haven't seen the third floor yet, and then there's the carriage house in the back."

"A carriage house?"

"It's a four-car garage with storage on the main level and a large apartment above it. Come. We can see it from the back bedroom."

He held my right hand, and I hung onto his arm with my left.

"See?" he said, pointing out the window.

I'd never seen more than the front of the house, but in the back, there was playground equipment that looked similar to what was in the park. "What's that?" I asked, pointing at a small structure beneath a huge, old white pine.

"I think it might've been a playhouse."

After looking at the third floor, Tackle led me down to the main level and into the kitchen. He opened up a cupboard and pulled out a roll of paper. He removed the rubber band and spread it out on the counter.

"This is the front of the house. My dad and I believe that, at one time, there were two large covered porches off each side of the portico. They must've been ripped off the main structure. I intend to put them back." He rested his finger on another part of the drawing, this time on the side of the house. "I think this may have been a sunroom or sleeping porch. Another porch stretches across the back of the house, big enough that it could be made into two more rooms or left as an outdoor living area since it looks out over the backyard."

"This must've cost a fortune," I muttered.

He shook his head. "There was an auction. It went for not much more than the back taxes."

"But the cost to renovate it must be staggering."

Tackle shrugged. "Not so much when your family owns a construction company."

"I don't know what to say."

He crowded me against the counter and put a hand on either side of me. "Don't say anything yet. Just tell me you'll try to keep an open mind."

I gripped the counter when the dizziness got worse. I knew I was about to lose consciousness when I felt my legs give out, and Tackle caught me.

24

Tackle

Sloane was only unconscious long enough for me to pick her up and carry her into the dining room. I'd just sat down on the window seat, the only place in the house where we could sit, when her eyes opened.

A thousand thoughts raced through my mind in those few seconds. Should I call 9-1-1? How far away was Cowboy? Should I text him and ask him to come inside? Was Sloane getting enough to eat? Enough rest? Had I worn her out by bringing her here? I thought back to last night and how little sleep either of us had gotten. I had to be more careful about that in the future.

Or was there something in the house that had made her pass out? It was so old. Had I brought her into a place that might be toxic for her and the baby?

"How do you feel?" I asked when I looked into her beautiful blue eyes.

"I must've passed out."

"That, you did. Do you have any idea what brought it on?"

"I was feeling dizzy."

"Didn't think it was important to mention that to me?" When I smiled, so did she. "I'm overwhelming you."

When Sloane didn't say anything, I laughed. "I'll take that as silent affirmation." She tried to stand, but I wouldn't let her off my lap. "When's the last time you ate?"

"Earlier?"

"Today? This week?"

"Today."

"What sounds good? The Farmstead? Paddy's?"

She perked up at one of the two; I couldn't tell which. "I haven't been to Paddy's in ages."

"Do you feel good enough to walk or—"

"I feel fine. I passed out. Not a big deal."

"Not a big deal at all. People do it every day. It's especially not a big deal if it happens when they're driving. Or crossing the street at a busy intersection. Or in the shower."

"Oh my God, *stop*."

When I pulled up to the Irish restaurant that had been a Newton institution for as long as the grill had, something felt off to me. I could see in the rearview Cowboy park his truck a few spots over from where I was. I watched as he got out and walked over to the entrance. I waited for an all-clear sign before taking Sloane inside. It never came.

"What's going on?" she asked when Cowboy came back out and touched the right side of the brim of his hat instead.

"Let's go somewhere else."

Sloane folded her arms. "Did you think I didn't notice him?"

"Who?"

"The guy you've had following me. You know, the one who just went into Paddy's, came back out, and signaled you not to go inside."

I shook my head and laughed. "So is Farmstead okay with you instead?"

"Of course."

We drove up and went through the same routine we had at the last place. This time, I saw Cowboy give the all clear.

"What's his name?" asked Sloane when we got out of the car.

"Garrison Cassidy."

"Good Lord. Where'd you find him? Texas?"

"He's one of Doc's finds."

When we walked inside, Cowboy was seated at the counter studying a menu.

"Ask him to join us," Sloane said before the hostess approached.

"How many?" she asked.

I said two and Sloane said three.

"Three and a half," I joked when the woman went to clear a table.

"More like three and a third."

The hostess motioned for us to follow. Once Sloane was seated, I went to get Cowboy.

"What was the deal at Paddy's?" I asked.

"See for yourself." He held out his phone, and I looked at the photo he'd taken.

"Is that DeLuca?" The very guy who Razor said was purported to be the head of the Sabatino family and who Nick's husband had alleged connections to.

"Affirmative."

"Do you think his being on this side of town is a coincidence?"

"I don't know, but I made Doc and Razor aware of his twenty."

"Good."

"Uh, how's Sloane?"

"Shit. Waiting for us." I motioned for him to follow me. "Whatever you do, do *not* mention DeLuca."

He gave me a "what do you take me for, asshole?" look.

"Hey, I'm Sloane. It's nice to meet you in person," she said when we joined her at the table.

"Garrison, but most call me Cowboy."

"So, Garrison, what did you see at Paddy's that made you divert us?"

Cowboy looked at me.

"Someone with connections to the Sabatino family was there," I answered for him.

"So?"

"Not the best place for former agency and current DHS," Cowboy responded.

"Got it." Sloane looked at something on the menu and then back at Cowboy. "Who was it?"

"Um..." He looked at me.

"Cadillac DeLuca," I answered for him a second time.

Sloane looked at me and then at Cowboy. "Would you please excuse us?"

"Of course." He got up and went back into the other room and sat at the counter.

"Who was it, Tackle?"

"I told you. DeLuca."

Sloane threw her menu on the table. "Take me home."

"What? No. You need to eat."

"And I will. At home. And not with someone who's lying to me." She shook her head. "Good job, by the way. You made it almost twenty-four hours before pulling another stunt that makes me unable to trust you."

Explaining why we'd avoided DeLuca meant I would have to divulge the connection between him, Caruso, and ultimately, Nick. Sloane would think I'd lied because I had some kind of involvement with her. I'd have no chance to explain the situation between Nick and her husband or what role I'd played in their lives.

"Please reconsider at least eating."

Sloane rested her forearms on the table and leaned forward. "You have three choices. Either you take me home, Cowboy takes me home, or I call a car service."

I stood and pulled her chair out.

"Good decision," she muttered.

Neither of us spoke on our way from the restaurant back to her place. Anything I might chance saying would only make the lie worse.

"Don't get out," she said when I pulled into the driveway.

"I'm coming in with you."

"No. I don't want you to."

"You passed out less than thirty minutes ago. I'm not leaving you alone."

"Take me to my parents' house instead."

I eyed the outfit she was wearing; it didn't do a thing to hide her tummy. "How do you plan to explain that?" I pointed to her midsection.

"That isn't your concern."

"Can we please go inside for a minute?"

"I'm going inside; you aren't."

I took a deep breath and let it out slowly, hoping I wasn't making an already bad decision worse.

"Cadillac DeLuca is the head of the Sabatino Crime Syndicate, who Dan Caruso, Claudette Caruso's husband, works for."

She looked at me with scrunched eyes.

"Nick."

Sloane didn't hesitate. She got out of the car and slammed the door behind her. She raced to her front door, but I got there ahead of her.

"Let me explain."

"Too late." She took her keys out of her purse. "Get out of my way."

I didn't want to have this conversation out in the open, but she was giving me no choice.

"He beat her up. That's what the deal was when she came into Max & Millie's the day you, Halo, and I were there for lunch. She asked for my help."

"*Your* help. There was no one else she could go to? The police, for example?"

"Sloane, please, I don't want to talk about this out on the front stoop."

She hesitated, but opened the door, and I followed her inside.

"Caruso is a bad dude, and Sabatino is worse." I walked into the kitchen and opened the refrigerator.

"What are you doing?"

"Looking for something to eat."

"Help yourself. What's mine is yours." She had a disgusted look on her face and shook her head.

"For you."

"I'm perfectly capable of finding my own food."

I ignored her, took a jar of raspberry jam out of the fridge, and opened cabinets until I found bread, peanut butter, and plates. I made two sandwiches and handed one to her.

While she ate, I explained that I'd put Nick up in an apartment so she was safe and how I'd gone to K19 for help in getting her protection. I also told her how Razor Sharp had somehow gotten enough on her husband to get him picked up and put in jail.

"I have no idea if DeLuca knows anything about it, and if he does, whether he gives a shit. According to Razor, his plan was to set it up so Cadillac believed Caruso planned to turn state's evidence."

"What's your involvement with this woman?"

"I have none. We dated a few times in high school. That's it."

Sloane shook her head. "Doesn't add up."

"What doesn't?"

"Why she came to you."

"Everyone we know, knows I worked for the agency. Some know I don't anymore. It isn't a stretch to think she'd come to me, Sloane."

"Knox thought she was the woman you were talking about when you said you weren't sure the person you were interested in was as into you as you were them."

"We've covered that. You were that person."

"Right. And I believe you because you haven't lied to me before."

"That isn't fair. I didn't lie to you."

She went into the kitchen and made a second sandwich. She pointed to the bread. "Want another?"

I ate the one I had in four bites. "Yes, please."

"This is why I was being watched. Caruso knows you helped his wife, and you being around me, puts me in danger."

"I'm not sure he knows, and I stayed away until I believed there was no longer a threat."

"Now you think there's a threat from DeLuca?"

"I don't know."

"You need to leave."

"Sloane, come on. Don't do this."

"Until you know whether you're putting me and our baby at risk by being here, you can't be around us."

I understood. I didn't like it, but she was right. It was the reason I'd stayed away in the first place. "I don't like you being here on your own with Halo out of town."

"I'll go to my parents'."

"I'll take you."

"Good idea. That way, I won't be safe there either, and neither will they."

"Okay. I won't take you, but I will be arranging for more detail." I had another idea brewing in the back of my mind, but until I had everything in place, I wouldn't bring it up to Sloane. "If you're going to tell them you're pregnant, I want to be there."

"I wasn't there when you told your mother."

"Are you going to tell them I'm the father?"

"No."

That hurt, and I couldn't explain why. I'd known for less than twenty-four hours, and yet, the baby was *mine*, and I wanted the world to know it.

Sloane's face softened. "I want to tell my parents and Knox that you're the father at the same time. With you there. If Knox was back from New York City, then maybe I'd do it today."

"Thank you."

"I'm sorry I'm angry, Tackle."

"I'm the one who's sorry."

"Okay, we're both sorry. You made me promise I'd tell you the truth. Is it really too much for me to expect the same of you?"

"Of course it isn't."

"If you want me to 'keep an open mind,' then you need to be honest with me. That includes telling me things I should know or that relate to me, in real time."

The fact that my mind was racing with what I hadn't yet told her that I should've, drove home how right she was.

"I want to turn the smaller bedroom on the second floor into a nursery for the baby," I blurted.

She walked over and handed me the other sandwich. We both sat on the sofa. When she put her plate on the coffee table, so did I.

"I love that idea," she said, turning her body to face mine.

"Does that mean—"

"It means I love the idea."

"Got it."

"I'm going to ask you a question, and I want you to tell me the truth."

"Shoot."

"Swear to me there isn't any kind of relationship whatsoever between you and Nick."

"There isn't." I said the words, but that didn't change the fact that Nick wanted there to be, no matter how much I didn't. What she wanted wouldn't sway me; I didn't want any other woman in my life other than Sloane, my mom, and our baby, if it was a girl.

"Was there one?"

"Not since high school. You asked me to swear, and I did."

I hated that Sloane looked like she didn't believe me, but I loved that she didn't tell me to leave again.

Two days later, Ranger called.

"What's up?" I asked.

"Nick is making noise about needing you to come back out here."

"Why?"

"You know why, Tackle."

"Tell her I said no."

"Already tried that."

"No means no, man. I'm not coming every time she calls. In fact, I'm never coming again. She needs to accept that."

"She's threatening to come there."

"Stop her."

"It isn't that simple. K19 arranged for a place for her to live and supplied her with a new identity, but she isn't under house arrest, Tackle. She isn't a prisoner. We've even cut back on surveillance."

"Tell her it's for her own safety that she not return to Massachusetts, at least until her husband goes to trial."

"Ex-husband now."

That in itself was a relief. It was pretty easy to get a divorce in Massachusetts. All one spouse had to do was cite irreconcilable differences. Even if Caruso had tried to contest it, unless Nick filed based on fault, the courts wouldn't allow it. The only holdup was the ninety-day waiting period.

"Ex or not, he could still have people on the lookout for her."

Ranger didn't reply.

"Listen, I'm involved with someone else now. It's serious, and I won't jeopardize that relationship because Nick believes I'm, somehow, her knight in shining armor."

"That news would be better coming straight from you."

Ranger was probably right. As much as I detested confrontation, I had to shut Nick down once and for all. I had to make her understand that there was no chance she and I would ever be together.

"All right. I'll talk to her." I'd blocked her from contacting me, even from the new phone K19 had supplied her with, so I didn't want to call her directly. "When will you be back at her place?"

"I'm sitting out front."

"All right, let's get this over with. Go inside and put me on speaker."

25

Sloane

"Where are you?" my brother asked when I answered his call.

"At the office. Where are you?"

"Just landed at Logan. Got time for lunch?"

It was almost two in the afternoon. I'd eaten lunch at eleven, but I was already hungry again, so I said yes. When Knox asked where we should meet, I gave him the name of the Mediterranean place where Tackle and I had eaten. Since it was at the public market, if my brother wanted something different, he had plenty of choices.

"Wow, look at you," he said when he saw me. "How long was I gone?"

"I know," I murmured, rubbing my belly. "Since it popped, it just keeps growing."

"Mom told me that you told her and Dad you were pregnant."

"I figured she would." It ended up not being a big deal when I sat the two of them down to tell them. My mom insisted she already knew, which I doubted. If she really had, she would've been fussing over me as much as she had been over the last week. My dad's face broke into a knowing smile, making me think he had truly suspected.

Knox went to get our food when they called our number.

"What did you want to talk to me about?" I asked when he sat back down.

He smiled, and his cheeks flushed. "Guessed it wasn't just lunch, then, huh?"

"Yep."

He took a bite of his food. "Damn, this place is really good. How'd you find it?"

"A friend and I came here."

Knox ate a few more bites and set his napkin on the table. "Mom is hounding me to tell her who the father is. She doesn't believe I don't know."

"She's hounding me too, but I doubt that's why you wanted to meet for lunch."

"You're right. Here goes. I want to move to New York City to live with Tara."

I jumped up and threw my arms around his neck. "That's such wonderful news. I'm so happy for you, Knox." I sat back down.

"I made the decision to talk to you about it after Mom called. I was hoping that, since they knew, you wouldn't be as uncomfortable with me being so far away."

"You did so much for me in the last several weeks; how could I deny you anything? But you're right. Now that our parents know, I don't feel so alone."

Not to mention that the baby's father was also in the picture. Soon, Knox and my parents would know it was Tackle. Very soon.

"When are you leaving?"

"As soon as I get my place packed up."

"So, tomorrow?" I laughed, but I knew my brother. He wasn't the kind of guy to accumulate a lot of possessions.

He laughed too. "Yeah, probably. I, uh, have something else to tell you."

"Okay."

"I asked Tara to marry me."

I jumped up for the second time and hugged him.

"It's going to happen kind of quick, which means her friends are hosting an engagement party for us next week. I hope you can be there."

"Of course I will be. I wouldn't miss it."

After lunch, Knox left to pack and tell our parents his news. I planned to join him in Newton, but decided to swing by the Chestnut Hill house first.

Sort of. I never went straight there. First, I stopped at the market and the drugstore. At each place, Cowboy made sure I didn't have a tail that I hadn't picked up on myself. Today, like every other day, when I got the all clear from him, I drove to the house and parked in the garage.

"Hey, you," said Tackle when I came inside and found him waiting for me in the kitchen. "Hungry?"

"No, I met Knox for a late lunch." He dished himself a bowl of pasta that smelled so good I was tempted to eat again. I followed him into the dining room that was now furnished, as were most of the other rooms in the house. The parlor was one of the only ones on the main floor that wasn't, since we were waiting to tell Knox about the house and that Tackle was my baby's father before we moved the furniture over that was in my side of the duplex.

"He called, and I told him I'd see him at his place later."

"Oh." We'd been sleeping at the Chestnut Hill house every night since the bedroom furniture had been delivered.

"I thought it might be a good idea if you stayed at your place tonight too, just in case he comes by, looking for you."

"That makes sense."

"Sorry about this."

"Don't be. I think he's planning on leaving as soon as tomorrow anyway."

"One of the reasons I'm meeting him. I'm part of the box-loading muscle team. I'd say that I'd sneak over to your place, but I have a feeling we'll be back at it pretty early tomorrow morning."

I leaned over and rested my head on Tackle's shoulder. "I'm not ready to tell him."

He kissed my forehead. "I'm not either."

That surprised me. "Why not?"

"He and Tara haven't been back together very long. I'd rather let him have time to think about her and only her."

"You're a good friend to him."

"I'd be willing to bet that's your reason too."

I smiled. "It is."

He went in to get another bowl of pasta and came back with one for me too.

"You're a good guy, Tackle."

"I'm trying, Sloane. I don't think I've ever tried so hard in my life."

The next morning, I was headed to my parents' house to go shopping for baby stuff with my mom when I got a call from Tackle.

"Miss me already?"

"Always, but, um, there's something I need to talk to you about."

"Okay."

"Your brother just left. Can you swing by here?"

"Sure. I'm just on my way to my parents'."

"I know, peanut."

"Knox is calling me."

"See you in a minute."

I pressed accept on the touchscreen. "Hey, Knox."

"I just passed you. Did you need something?"

"What do you mean?"

"Are you headed to my place?"

"Oh! Uh, no. Just meeting a friend for lunch."

"Okay, well, see you next week."

"Yep."

"God, I missed you last night," Tackle said when he opened my car door and offered his hand.

I climbed out and kissed him. "What did you need to talk to me about?"

"Let's go inside."

I followed him in and sat on a step stool.

"Can I get you anything?"

"You can get to the point of why I'm here."

"I got a call from Doc. He's asked me to fly to California."

"For?"

"There's something going down that he needs my help with."

I clenched my fists. "Would you just tell me?"

"Nick has issued an ultimatum of sorts. He's asked me to fly out and smooth it over. I should only be gone a couple of days."

"I see."

"If it was anyone but Doc..."

"I get it. When do you have to leave?"

"Tomorrow morning?"

"You aren't sure?"

"He asked me to let him know when I was planning to leave. I haven't yet."

I was annoyed about him having to fly to California to deal with an ex-girlfriend's temper tantrum; however, I understood it took guts for her to leave the abusive situation she'd been in. If she needed Tackle's support to see it through, not allow herself to get pulled back into a toxic relationship, I could be supportive.

"Tomorrow would be better than today," I said, which made him wiggle his eyebrows. I didn't want to ask, but I had to. "There's nothing between the two of you, right?"

Tackle took a deep breath and let it out slowly.

"You're fucking kidding me—"

"Hang on. Let me answer your question."

"I'm not sure I want to hear it."

"There is nothing between Nick and me."

"Why did it take you so long to answer if that's the case?"

"Because she wants there to be and she's relentless. Now, before you start swearing at me again, know that I have less than zero percent interest in her. None. I've made it clear to her again and again that nothing will happen between her and me, now or in the future."

"Does she know about me?"

"She knows there's someone in my life."

"Does she know I'm pregnant?" God, I hated having to ask all these questions. Why was he weighing his answers so carefully? It was almost as though he was dancing around the truth. "Spit it out. I'm running out of patience."

"I may have let it slip."

"Tackle? What the fuck?"

"She was threatening to leave California and come back to Boston if I didn't come to her. Instead, I had a conversation with her over the phone."

"And?"

"And, like I told you before, I made it clear that nothing will happen between her and me. Not now or in the future."

"Because I'm pregnant?"

"When she suggested the relationship I was in wouldn't last, I told her it would."

"Because of the baby?"

"That's what I told her. It isn't the way I feel."

"Is this what the ultimatum is about? Me?"

"She told Doc she wanted to leave. And here's the deal. We can't force her to stay in California." He explained that she wasn't a prisoner or even under any kind of house arrest. "It's in her best interest to stay there, at least until Caruso stands trial and is sentenced. But if she wants to leave, no one can stop her."

"Do you believe she'd be in danger if she came back?"

"I do."

"I don't like this."

"I don't either, Sloane. Believe me. I told you before that if anyone other than Doc had asked, I would've said to tell Nick she was on her own if she didn't want to accept K19's help."

"You'd never forgive yourself if you did that and something happened to her."

"The other thing is, when I first discussed this with Doc, he told me his first wife had been in an abusive relationship before he married her. I got the impression it might have been the only reason he said it. Anyway, he wants me to try to talk her into staying where she is, so I will."

"Does she know you're coming?"

"Yes, but not when specifically."

"I'm going to call my mom and tell her I'd rather go shopping tomorrow."

"You're sure?"

"Positive."

I didn't sleep very well, so neither did Tackle. It was as though we both knew something bad was about to happen, and yet we kept reassuring each other that he'd be back in a couple of days, we'd go to Knox's engagement party, and if we felt the time was right, we'd tell him we were together. Once that happened, we'd both feel ready to move on with our lives.

"I'll call you when I land," he said when he walked me to my car the next morning. "Send me pictures of all the baby stuff you and your mom get today."

I laughed and waved as I drove away.

My mom said she'd pick me up at the duplex around noon. In the meantime, I planned to pack up more of my stuff, do some laundry, and maybe even try to take a nap.

I woke up when I heard someone knocking on my front door. I rolled over and picked up my phone to check the time. It sure didn't feel like I'd been asleep as long as I had.

"Huh," I said out loud. It was only a little after ten. What was my mom doing here so early? I flung the door open to ask, and instead of my mother, Tackle's ex-girlfriend was standing on my front stoop, and she looked to be about as pregnant as I was.

26

Tackle

"What do you mean she isn't here?" I asked Ranger when my flight landed and I called him after seeing a message from him.

"Hey, Tackle. How are you?"

"Fuck off. Answer my question. I just flew all the way across the country to talk to Nick, and now you're telling me she isn't here?"

"Here's what I know. Diesel stopped by her place this morning to check in, and she wasn't there."

"Are you watching her?"

"Not all the time. I told you we backed off on surveillance."

I got it. Around-the-clock detail was expensive, particularly when there was no known threat. "Are you tracking her?"

"Negative. Come on, Tackle, think. We gave her a new identity, a place to live, and even tried to get her a job. There isn't any reason for us to track her."

"Copy that. Any idea how long she's been gone or where she might be?"

"Negative."

"You said you tried to get her a job. Could she be at work?"

Ranger laughed. "Emphasis on the word tried. She didn't last a day. The other thing to note is the woman isn't typically out of bed before ten, so the fact that she was already gone this morning made Diesel think she hadn't just run to the store."

"When did he stop by?"

"Two hours ago, and she hasn't returned."

"I guess I should call Doc."

"That would be my advice."

"Thanks, Ranger, and sorry about snapping at you."

"I get it."

"Tackle," said Doc when he answered my call. "I just got word from Diesel that Claudette Caruso has vanished."

Vanished? That was a strong word. While Diesel seemed to think the woman wouldn't leave the house that early in the morning, there was still the possibility she was out running errands…or something.

"Have you attempted contact?" Doc asked.

"Not yet. I just landed, talked to Ranger, and called you."

"Copy that. See if you can get her to respond to you."

"Will do." I hung up and called the number of the phone K19 had provided to her. As much as I didn't want her to have my number, this time I had no choice. It went straight to voicemail.

No luck, read the text I sent to Doc. *Headed to her place now.*

Copy that, he responded.

27

Sloane

I had so many questions, I didn't know where to begin. "What are you doing here?" I blurted.

"Can I come in?"

"Whatever you have to say to me, you can say from where you are."

"Okay, if that's how you want to play this."

"I don't want to play anything, so either say what you have to say or leave."

"As you can see, Landry has been a very busy boy." She waved her hand at her stomach and mine. "I came to appeal to you, woman to woman, to let him go so he could do the right thing and be a part of our child's life, but I see now that you might want to ask the same thing of me."

"You already knew I was pregnant."

"I can assure you, I did not."

"Tackle already told me he told you. There's nothing for us to discuss."

"Interesting that you believe he told me about you when he obviously didn't tell you about me."

I knew she was attempting to goad me into asking if the baby really was Tackle's, and I had no intention of falling into her trap.

"You don't think the baby is his, do you?"

"Who the father of my baby is, is none of your business."

She smirked. "You know what I meant."

"We're done here." I got the door partway closed when she held up her phone.

"I can prove it to you. I'm sure he's frantic with worry since he flew all the way out to California to reassure me that he'd be there for me and our baby. I'll just give him a call, and you can hear for yourself."

I slammed the door before she could make good on her threat.

28

Tackle

"You're sure she knew I was coming?"

Ranger glared at me.

"Answer me, goddammit."

"Fuck off, Tackle."

"Yes or no?"

"I already told you she did. More than once."

"So where is she?"

"I wish I knew. Instead of me standing here while you grill me, wouldn't it make more sense for me to get out there and look for her?"

I picked up the keys to the rental.

"You should stay here in case she comes back."

After Ranger left, I called Sloane, who didn't pick up. It didn't surprise me since, by now, she would be shopping with her mom. I ended the call without leaving a message and called Nick, like I had been every fifteen minutes since I landed and Ranger told me she wasn't at the house K19 had set her up in. This time, she answered.

"Nick? Where the hell are you?"

"I'm in Chicago."

"Chicago? What the fuck are you doing there?"

"Why are you swearing at me?"

"Cut the innocent act. You knew I was coming here to see you, at your demand, I might add."

"No one told me you were coming to California, so I was on my way to you."

"In Chicago?"

"I had a layover. That's when I got Ranger's message that you were there."

I didn't believe a word she was saying, and I was getting angrier by the minute. "What's it gonna be? Are you getting on a plane and flying back to California, or should I tell Doc and the other guys that you've decided to wing this on your own?"

"Calm down, Landry. I'll catch the next flight out I can get."

I ended the call and immediately called Sloane. Not only did I want to hear her voice, I had to warn her that Nick and I had crossed paths in the sky and I'd probably be here another day at least. I left a message when the call went straight to voicemail.

If you see Sloane, tell her I'm trying to reach her, read the text I sent to Cowboy three hours later.

Roger that, he responded.

When I still hadn't been able to reach her an hour later, I called him. "Have you talked to Sloane?"

"No."

"Where is she?"

"Out with her mom and dad."

"Her mom *and* dad? Where?"

"They didn't tell me where they were going."

"She was supposed to be shopping with her mom."

"She was. When they got back, they left again, this time with her dad."

"When's the last time you saw them?"

"A couple of hours ago."

"You're supposed to be on her detail, Cowboy."

"What the hell, Tackle? Her dad told me to take the rest of the day off and get back to the job site. What was I supposed to do?"

"You didn't think to run that past me?"

"I don't work for you."

Since he was right, I didn't bother calling back when he hung up on me.

I spent the next hour trying to come up with a reason to call either of Sloane's parents to tell her to turn her damn phone on. By then, Ranger was back with Nick, and she didn't look the least bit contrite. He, though, looked ready to kill.

"I don't know why you're so mad," she said to him. "It was a simple misunderstanding."

"You *knew* Tackle was on his way here, and don't try to play it off like you didn't."

"I'm telling you, I didn't."

When I saw the veins in his neck bulge, I stepped between them. "Why don't you head out? I can take it from here."

Instead of immediately turning to leave, he looked at Nick.

"It's fine. Go."

He nodded and walked out.

"What was that all about?" I asked her once the door closed behind him.

"Nothing."

I got the feeling there was something up between her and Ranger but doubted either one would give me a straight answer about it.

"Let's talk," I said, motioning to the living room.

When she sat on the sofa, I took a seat in one of the chairs.

"Nick, I'm going to say this one more time and then that's it. I got you away from Caruso, even worked it so the asshole went to jail with the help of Doc and the other guys. But now, I'm done. You're safe, and I have my own life to lead."

"I should never have agreed to come to California. I hate it here." She studied her fingernails and then looked back up at me. "I'm bored out of my mind. I want to go home."

"You're the one who told me your husband had 'connections,' Nick. Have you forgotten that?"

"He's in jail, Tackle. He can't hurt me from there."

"You don't think any one of those *connections* would be capable of carrying out his wishes while he's on the inside?"

She shrugged. "None of my friends are here, neither is my family."

"Make new friends."

"I'm not interested in new friends. I want to go back to Boston."

"If that's what you really want to do, I can't stop you. But I'll warn you, if you do, you'll be on your own. No coming to me for help. I'm not doing this again, Nick."

"I've made up my mind."

"Okay, we'll fly back together tomorrow."

Nick smiled and clapped her hands. "Perfect."

"One of the guys will bring you to the airport. I'll meet you there."

"Wait. Why do you have to leave?"

"I have other matters to take care of while I'm here. I'll see you tomorrow."

The smile left her face, and she didn't clap again. I really didn't give a shit. I'd talk to Doc, let him know she was leaving against my advice, and that would be that.

29

Sloane

"What about your place in Newton?" my mom asked when I told her and my dad that I wanted to move into Boston.

"The commute is getting harder on me. Besides, it's month to month."

My father hadn't said much, which was never a good sign. What he did say, confirmed my dread.

"It's time you told us the real reason, Sloane."

I took a deep breath and let it out slowly. "You aren't going to like this, and after I tell you, remember that I am an adult capable of making my own decisions."

My mother looked between my father and me. "You're worrying me, *mija*."

"Tackle is the baby's father."

My mother's face turned so pale I thought she might pass out. "*Oh Dios mío,*" she muttered, crossing herself. I wanted to ask her the last time she went to church, but that wasn't what this conversation was about.

I met my father's eyes and saw no surprise in them, although he was trained not to react. Maybe what I said next would tip him over the edge. "I have reason to believe I'm not the only woman pregnant with his child."

"*No!*" gasped my mother.

My dad nodded, but otherwise, had no visible reaction other than to brush his lips with his finger.

"Why do you think this, Sloane?" my mother asked.

"Because the other woman showed up at my house."

"You're certain that this woman's child is his?"

"Certain? No, but I have reason to believe she wasn't lying."

"Have you asked him, *mija*?"

I looked at my father, wishing he would jump in on this conversation, but evidently, he'd gone mute.

"What are you thinking?" I asked him.

"I'm not certain yet." He cleared his throat. "Does your brother know?"

I shook my head, and my eyes filled with tears. My mother reached over and pulled me into an embrace. "It will be okay, Sloane. Shh, everything will be okay."

"I can't talk to Tackle," I said through my tears.

"You don't have to, *mija*," she said, stroking my hair.

"What do you want to do?" my father asked.

"I want to stay in the city for a few days until I figure things out."

He raised a brow.

"I'm not running away. I just need time to think."

"Where's Tackle now?"

"That's the thing, Dad. He's on the other side of the country, with *her*."

He nodded. "A few days to think things through, peanut. If this baby is his, you can't avoid him forever."

"There's more you should know."

"Go ahead."

I told both my parents about the house Tackle and his father had bought in Chestnut Hill and about how he was renovating it for us to live in. I also told them about how, as soon as he learned I was pregnant, he'd immediately wanted to get married. My mother's eyes perked up.

"Don't get your hopes up, Mom. I'm not marrying him. Not that he asked. He just told me we'd get married."

My dad smiled. "Sounds like him."

"Don't you go soft on him. Evidently, he decided after almost dying in a plane crash to impregnate women all over the country."

"Like your mother said, everything will be okay, peanut."

"Oh, and his mother knows."

My mother's eyes opened wide. "*What?*"

"He told her without asking me first."

With my assurance that I wouldn't avoid Tackle indefinitely, my father got me a furnished apartment in the North End.

"Are you sure you don't want to stay with us?" my mother asked.

"No, Mom. I need to be where he can't force me to talk to him until I'm ready."

"Ben, do you think this is a good idea?"

My father put his arm around my mother's shoulders. "Yes, sweetheart, or I wouldn't have made arrangements for the apartment."

The way he looked at her tore at my heart. Even when they were arguing, the love he had for her was so obvious. For the last couple of weeks, I'd let myself believe that maybe one day, Tackle would feel that way about me. How could I have been so stupid?

30

Tackle

By the time the flight landed, I was filled with dread. Cowboy assured me he'd confirmed Sloane spent the afternoon and evening with her parents. However, when they returned home, she wasn't with them. He'd checked the duplex in Newton and the house in Chestnut Hill, and she wasn't at either.

Finally, I gave him the address of Sloane's friend's apartment and asked him to check there. Her friend was home but insisted she hadn't seen Sloane since before Thanksgiving.

I knew she'd be furious with me if I went to either Halo or her parents, but I was reaching the point where I had to. Given her mom and dad were the last to see her, according to Cowboy, I decided to pay them a visit rather than call Knox.

"I wish you all the best," I said to Nick when we got off the plane.

"What do you mean? You're not just leaving me here?"

"You have all your friends and family that you're so anxious to get back to. You should've planned for someone to pick you up."

"I just assumed you'd make sure I got home okay."

I took Nick by the arm and led her off to the side of the terminal area. "I told you before we left California that if you made this decision, you'd be on your own. I meant it. I did everything I could to get you out of an abusive situation and relocated to a place your ex-husband couldn't find you. You decided that wasn't good enough, so I'm done."

"But—"

"No, Nick. I'm done." I stalked away without looking back and hopped on the shuttle that would take me to the private lot where I'd left my car. I tried Sloane's number again from the shuttle and before I got on the road. Both times, it went straight to voicemail.

Something had happened to make her ghost me, and I had no idea what it could be. Before I left for California, I thought she understood why I had to go. She'd spent the night with me, we had the same amazing sex we always did, and the next morning, she gave me a kiss goodbye that promised more to come when I got back.

Why wouldn't she have just been honest with me if she was that angry about me going? She had every opportunity to either tell or show me how she really felt.

I shook my head. That couldn't be it. Something else had to have happened. I called my mom.

"Hello, sweetheart," she said, answering my call.

"I have to ask you a question."

"Go ahead."

"You didn't tell Sloane's parents I'm her baby's father, did you?"

"Of course I didn't. You know I wouldn't do that, which means you have a good reason for asking."

"I went on a quick work trip. When I left, I thought everything was okay between us, but I haven't been able to reach her since that morning."

"Landry, you don't think something's happened to her, do you?"

"No, I mean, someone I know saw her yesterday, and she was fine."

"Where did this person see her?"

"She was with Ben and Carolina."

"I see. And you can't very well ask them, can you?"

"I don't think I have any choice."

"I will do this once, Landry, but only once."

"Do what?"

"I'll pay them a visit and see if I can find anything out."

"Mom, don't—"

"I will not tell them a thing. I'll just casually ask after her. I have to talk to Carolina about the plans for Knox's engagement party anyway."

"Are you going?"

"Of course we are. We wouldn't miss it."

"Who's we?"

"Your father and me? Remember him?"

"I can't believe Dad agreed to go."

"It's in New York City, Landry. We're making a week of it."

"Are Sloane's parents too?"

"I don't know, darling, but it's the excuse I'm using to pay them a visit."

Not knowing what else to do with myself, I drove to the Chestnut Hill house. Maybe I'd find some clue as to what was going on with Sloane.

I'd been sitting on the porch, staring off at nothing for at least a half hour when my phone rang.

"Hey, Mom."

"They know you're the father, Landry. Evidently, Sloane told them. They don't seem upset about it, but they didn't see the need to keep up any pretenses."

"Is she okay?"

"They didn't say otherwise."

"Did you ask?"

"No, I completely forgot. *Of course* I asked, Landry."

"Okay, sorry."

"One thing happened that seemed odd."

"What's that?"

"Carolina walked me to the door and said it's time we all went out for Italian again. And then she suggested we make a night of it and go back to Dominici in the North End."

"Why is that odd?"

"Two things, unless I'm losing my memory, we've never eaten at Dominici either with the Clarksons or alone."

"What's the other thing?"

"Carolina was whispering when she said it. She even looked over her shoulder once as though she was checking to see if Ben could hear her."

When I was still wide awake at four in the morning, I figured I might as well drive to Little Italy.

31

Sloane

When I opened my eyes, I knew I was on the floor. Otherwise, nothing looked familiar to me. Something was wrong, really wrong. I had to get to my phone, but I couldn't remember where I'd left it.

I tried to raise my head, but God, it hurt. My head was throbbing—pounding—so hard it was impossible to think.

Cramps. It wasn't just my head; my stomach hurt as well. The cramping was so bad that I tried to wrap my arms around my midsection, but they felt so heavy.

I inched one hand down and felt something damp. What was that? I looked. Blood. The baby.

Oh my God, the baby.

"Help!" I tried to shout, knowing there was no one close enough to hear me.

32

Tackle

I'd been walking for almost two hours with absolutely no idea of what I hoped to find. I concentrated my efforts on the block where the Dominici restaurant was located, but traipsed around neighboring streets too.

One by one, coffee shops and bakeries were rolling up their steel gates, turning on lights, and dragging tables and chairs out to the sidewalk. I checked my phone. It was almost six: the time most of them officially opened.

Even if the bizarre conversation my mother had had with Carolina meant that Sloane was staying somewhere near Dominici, I had no idea how I'd be able to find her.

I stared up at the buildings surrounding me. Each one was filled with either office suites or luxury apartments above the street-level shops. Each might have as many as a hundred living spaces, particularly the ones with thirty stories or more.

"Sloane, where the hell are you?" I muttered out loud, scanning the high-rises as if she'd come out on the balcony of one and I'd spot her.

"You're too early if you're looking for Sloane," said a kid sweeping the sidewalk in front of a coffeehouse.

"You know somebody by that name?"

"Really pretty, stomach out to here?" The kid, who couldn't be more than ten or eleven, held his hand out in front of him.

Rather than respond, I took the photo I'd brought with me out of my pocket. "This her?" I asked, handing it to him.

"Yep. That's Sloane."

"Have you seen her?"

"I did the last two days."

"Where?"

"Here," the kid said, laughing as he swept dirt onto the street. "Comes down for breakfast, but not until later."

"What time?"

He shrugged. "Not before nine or ten, after the morning rush is over."

"You said she comes downstairs. Does she live in this building?"

"Anthony!" a man yelled.

"I gotta go. See ya, mister."

"Hey, wait!" I was too late. The kid was inside with the door closed behind him.

I waited another twenty minutes and went into the shop.

"*Buongiorno,*" said an older woman, who didn't look quite tall enough to see over the counter. "What can I get you this morning?"

"*Un caffè, per favore.*"

The woman smiled. "*Parla italiano?*"

"Enough to order coffee."

"What else? *Sfogliatelle* maybe?"

"Too rich for me this morning. How about a brioche?"

She put my pastry in a bag and turned to make my *caffè*.

"There was a young boy sweeping the sidewalk earlier, Anthony?"

"*Sì,* my grandson."

"Is he here?"

"He's at school now."

"He mentioned a woman, Sloane. He said she came here for breakfast the last couple of days."

The woman turned around and studied me. "Who are you?"

"A good friend of hers."

She shook her head. "I don't know her."

I pulled the same photo out that I'd shown the boy. "Are you sure you haven't seen her?" I asked, handing it to her.

Before she could respond, we heard sirens. I turned toward the window and saw an ambulance pull up near the door that led to the building's elevators.

I tossed a twenty on the counter and raced out. "I'm a trained first responder," I shouted. "Can I help?"

"Woman called 9-1-1," one of the paramedics answered. "Bleeding. Maybe a miscarriage."

I gripped the rail in the elevator after he motioned for me to get on, and counted every ding as it seemed to take ten minutes to reach the twentieth floor.

"This way," one of them shouted, rushing down the hallway.

"Paramedics," one of the guys shouted, pounding on the door.

"Did the victim give a name?" I asked one of the other guys.

He looked at his phone. "Sloane?"

I pushed the guy standing at the door out of the way and slammed my body into it. It swung open, and I raced over to where I saw Sloane's crumpled body on the floor.

"Don't move her!" shouted one of the other guys.

"She's pregnant. About six months," I shouted back, checking the vitals of the unconscious woman I loved with every fiber of my being.

"I got a pulse," said one of the other guys. "A lot of blood," he muttered, motioning with his head. "You know her?"

"I'm the baby's father." They were about to lift her onto the gurney when Sloane opened her eyes.

"Tackle?"

"Hi, peanut." I leaned down and kissed her forehead. "We're gonna get you over to the hospital."

"The baby?"

"The baby is going to be fine, and so are you."

"We are?"

"Yep."

"How...how did you find me?" Her eyes closed, and her head fell to the side.

"Who's this guy?" asked one of the men who'd stayed with the ambulance when I went to get in with her.

"The baby's father," answered the EMT who'd checked her pulse.

"Ride up front," said the first guy.

"He's a first responder."

"Quit arguing and let's go!" shouted the driver.

I got in, the door slammed closed, and I took Sloane's hand in mine.

A woman in a white coat opened the curtain and walked over to the bed in the emergency room bay. "She lost a lot of blood, but every test we ran indicated the baby is fine. I understand you're the father?"

"That's right."

"I'm Dr. Phillips, and this is Audrey, the tech who will do the ultrasound." The woman wheeled a large cart in behind her.

"Hello, Sloane. I'm Dr. Phillips. We're going to take a peek at your baby."

I squeezed the hand I'd been holding and leaned down to kiss her forehead. "It's nice to see those beautiful blue eyes looking back at me."

"You're here."

The tech moved the blanket and sheet back and folded the hospital gown the nurses had changed her into while she'd slipped in and out of consciousness.

She spread gel on her tummy, and Sloane hissed. "That's cold."

"Sorry," the tech mumbled.

The screen was turned in such a way that neither Sloane nor I could see it, but the tech and doctor could.

"Do you know whether you're having a boy or a girl?" Dr. Phillips asked.

"No," Sloane answered.

"Do you want to know?"

She looked up at me.

"It's up to you, peanut."

She bit her bottom lip, and I leaned in closer. "If you want to wait, it's okay with me," I whispered.

"I want to know," she whispered back.

The doctor repositioned the machine so we could see the screen.

"Oh, wow," I gasped, gazing at the tiny human appearing in 3D. I could even see his or her face. I looked down at Sloane, whose eyes were filled with tears.

"It's amazing, isn't it?" she murmured.

I brushed at the moisture forming at the corner of my eye. "Miraculous."

"Last time I'll ask. Are you sure you want to know?"

I looked at Sloane, who nodded.

"Based on what I see, or don't see here,"—she pointed to the screen—"I'd say you're having a little girl."

I didn't care if Sloane was mad at me, not speaking to me, whatever it was that made her hide from me, I leaned down and kissed her lips. "Congratulations, little mama."

Sloane brought her arm up, wrapped it around my neck, and I kissed her again.

When the tech left, the doctor pulled a chair near the side of the gurney. "The bleeding you experienced was caused by placenta previa. Are you familiar with the term?"

Both Sloane and I shook our heads.

"In simpler terms, it means the placenta is either fully or partially covering the cervix. In your case, it's between full and partial. Three-quarters, if you will. I'm not concerned about you carrying the baby to full term, but in order to do that, you'll have to remain on bed rest for the duration."

"Okay," I heard Sloane whisper.

"I want to keep you overnight, just to be sure, but you should be able to return home tomorrow."

"Okay," she repeated.

"Any questions?" The doctor looked from me to Sloane and back again. I had a million but doubted she was looking for anything unrelated to what she'd just told us. "No? We'll see about getting you up to a regular room as soon as possible. I'll be back by later, either here or there, but hopefully there."

When the doctor left and pulled the curtain closed behind her, Sloane closed her eyes.

I stroked her hair. "Get some rest, peanut."

"Tackle, I..."

"Shh. Just rest for now. I'll be here when you wake up."

"My parents..."

"They're here. I called them. Do you want me to have them come in?"

"Not yet." Her eyes drifted closed again. "Tackle, you and I need to—"

I kissed her to stop her from talking. Whatever we needed to do, didn't need to be done right now. My guess was she wanted to talk about whatever it was that had made her hide from me.

The longer I sat by her side and watched her sleep, the more I realized I would do whatever I had to, to keep her in my life.

I'd already severed ties with Nick, but if that wasn't enough, I was ready to do whatever would be.

I think I may have dozed off when I heard the bay's curtain open.

"Tackle? What are you doing here?"

When I stood, I woke Sloane up. "Halo, um, did your parents call you?"

"My parents? No, I'm Sloane's ICE."

"Huh?"

"My number is listed on Sloane's phone in case of emergency."

"Oh. Right. Your parents should be in the waiting room."

"If my parents are here, why are you in with Sloane?" Halo went to the other side of the bed and leaned down to kiss his sister's forehead. "Hey, peanut, what happened?" he asked without waiting for me to answer his first question.

"Um..." She looked up at me.

"Something called placenta previa. Evidently, it causes bleeding. The baby is fine, though."

Halo looked from me to his sister. "Why isn't Mom in here with you?"

Sloane reached out and took my hand.

"Wait...no. No...fucking...way." Halo's face turned red, and his voice got louder with every word.

"Hang on," I said. "Let's take this conversation outside."

"You *sonuvabitch*," he seethed.

"Outside," I repeated, grabbing his arm and pulling him out of the bay. I picked up my pace, knowing this thing with Halo was going to escalate quickly. Whatever we had to say to each other, shouldn't be said in an emergency room full of people.

I went out the double doors the ambulance had pulled up to when they brought Sloane in, out to the parking lot, and stopped. Halo charged toward me, grabbing my shirt with one hand, and punching me in the face with the other.

"*You goddamn bastard. You got my little sister pregnant!*" he shouted, continuing to throw punches that I did little more than try to block.

"*Knox!*" I heard his father yell. "*Stop this! Now!*" His words did nothing to deter the man who had been my best friend for more than half my life from pummeling me. Only when Ben grabbed the back of Halo's collar and yanked him away from me, did he stop.

"You okay, man?" asked one of the paramedics I recognized from earlier. "Looks like he got you pretty good."

"I'm all right."

"Might be a couple gashes that need to be stitched up. Let's go in and take a look."

"I'll be fine."

The guy laughed. "Let's at least get you cleaned up, so you don't scare the shit out of that pretty girl you knocked up."

I laughed. "Okay, okay. I'll let you clean me up." I could already feel my right eye swelling up, and I knew my lip was split and bleeding.

33

Sloane

I looked at the bleeding knuckles on my brother's hand when he came back into the emergency room bay followed by my dad. "What did you do?"

"Less than I wanted to."

"Where's Tackle?"

"I think one of the paramedics is cleaning him up."

I looked from my father to my brother. "Cleaning him up? What the fuck, Knox?"

"Have a seat." My dad pulled out a chair and nudged Knox toward it. "The first thing the two of you need to do is lower your voices. There are other people in this hospital who are sick or injured and need care. They don't need to be disturbed by your argument."

"Argument?" I closed my eyes, took a deep breath, and told myself to calm down. "This isn't an argument, Dad. My brother just beat up the father of my baby."

"Don't call him that," Knox spat.

I'd never once seen my father lay a hand on my brother, until today. He didn't hit him hard, but he did swat the back of his head.

I, of course, did the most inappropriate thing ever and laughed out loud.

Knox spun around and looked at him. "Did you know?"

"I had my suspicions, as did your mother, but to answer your question; no, until recently, we did not know."

"That's why you wouldn't tell me who it was."

"You're right. If I could've kept it from you even longer, I would've. Do you want to know why?"

"Because you knew I'd kill him."

"No, Knox, because this isn't any of your business. Tackle and I are having a baby, and guess what? It has nothing to do with you. Nothing. This is between him and me and no one else. If you can't accept that, you can leave."

"Is he going to marry you?"

"The better question is, am I going to marry him? I haven't decided yet."

"You have to."

I stared at him, wide-eyed. "No wonder you're best friends. You're both Neanderthals. No, I don't have to."

"Is he at least going to take care of you and the baby? Provide for you?"

"Again, none of your business."

"I can't believe this."

"There isn't anything for you to believe. I'm pregnant, Tackle is the father, and the two of us will figure out how it's going to work in our own way."

"When did this happen?"

I looked up at my dad. "Would you please get him out of here?"

"We aren't finished talking about this."

"Yeah, Knox. We are. Go back to New York City." Those last words hurt him. I knew they did the minute I said them. I wasn't surprised by my brother's reaction. It was what I'd expected. I'd just hoped for better from him.

"Wait," I said when he stood to leave. "Dad, can you give us a minute?"

"I won't be far, and I better not be able to hear you."

"Sit back down, Knox," I said when my father pulled the curtain closed behind him. "You're not going to like what I'm about to tell you, but I want you to listen to me anyway."

He sat and folded his arms.

"Look at me." I waited until he raised his head. "I'm not a child, Knox. I'm a woman, as is evidenced by this." I put both hands on my belly. "Here's the part you're going to hate. I've loved Tackle since the day I met him. Head-over-heels loved him. I may not have understood the emotions I was feeling, but somewhere deep inside, I knew he was the only man I'd ever love. The only man I'd ever be with. Do you understand what I'm saying, Knox?"

"He took advantage of you, and for that—"

"That is the stupidest thing I've ever heard. Have you *met* me? Do you really believe that I would let *anyone* take advantage of me?"

I heard my dad clear his throat from the other side of the curtain and lowered my voice.

"I don't know if Tackle will ever feel the same way I do. I don't even know how much of a role he'll play in our baby's life. What I do know is that I'll still love him and I will never, ever regret having his baby. I haven't met her yet, but I love this little girl so much. I want you to be in her life. In order for me to allow that to happen, you have to promise me you'll take a step back, think about this from my point of view, and understand that none of this is about you."

"You're having a girl?"

I smiled. Of everything I'd said, that was the one thing I wanted him to focus on, and my brother hadn't disappointed me. I was having a baby girl, and she was all that really mattered.

"Knock, knock," I heard an unfamiliar voice say. The curtain opened, and a man in scrubs stepped in.

"I'm here to take you up to the fourth floor if you're ready."

"I'm ready."

"They're admitting you?" Knox asked.

"Just overnight. The doctor said she thinks I'll be able to go home tomorrow."

When the man wheeled me out, I looked around for Tackle, but didn't see him. "Um, wait," I said and he stopped. "Dad, do you know..."

He nodded. "I'll see if I can find him."

"Let me."

"Knox, please—"

"I need to, Sloane. He and I need to talk, and I promise not to use my fists this time."

"You promise?"

"I do."

34

Tackle

Halo didn't have to look far. I was in the bay next to Sloane. Ben knew it too, and I appreciated that he hadn't said anything.

I'd heard every word Sloane said, and a lot of them hurt worse than her brother's punches had.

Hearing her say she didn't know how much of a role I'd play in our baby's life almost killed me.

From the second I realized she was pregnant, I'd done everything I could to let her know I would be there for her and for the baby. Most of it, I didn't handle the right way, especially in the very beginning, but the time we'd spent together in the house in Chestnut Hill, I thought, had been magical.

I understood why she said she didn't know if I'd ever feel the same way about her as she felt for me. I'd never told her I loved her, but I did. I don't know exactly when I realized it. Maybe it wasn't until today, but I'd felt it.

When I heard Halo ask someone if they knew where I was, I got off the gurney and opened the curtain. "I'm right here."

"Oh, man." He winced. "Who did that to you?"

"Some asshole who believed he needed to defend the honor of his sister."

"She sure set me straight, didn't she?"

"In that way that only Sloane can." I followed him out of the emergency room and over to the bank of elevators.

"I'm sorry, Tackle."

"So am I."

"What for?"

"Mainly that we didn't tell you sooner. We wanted to, but then everything happened with Tara, and we decided to let you be happy for as long as we could."

"I'm not *unhappy*."

"I know. We just didn't want to put a damper on it. Ya know?"

"Yeah, I get it."

"So, that thing she said about whether or not she'd marry me? I kind of fucked that up big-time."

"What did you do?"

I spent the time we waited for the elevator and during the ride up to the fourth floor, telling him all the stupid shit I'd done since I found out Sloane was pregnant. When the doors opened, both Halo and I were laughing.

"I, uh, bought her a house. I mean, I didn't know I was buying it for her exactly when I did, but maybe I really did know."

"Huh?"

"Remember Chestnut Hill Park?"

"How could I forget it? It's where you broke my neck."

"You broke your neck. I didn't. Anyway, remember the house across the street and how whenever Sloane came along with us, she'd sit and stare at it?"

"Vaguely."

"You'll remember when you see it. My dad, the crew, and I have been renovating it. When you were first in New York with Tara, Sloane and I started living there."

"Wow."

"Yeah. It's pretty amazing."

"No, not wow the house; wow, you love her."

"Yeah, man, I do. Not that I've told her yet."

"Why not?"

"After all the bonehead things you did with Tara, you're giving me shit?"

"Oh Dios mío," Carolina said when I walked into Sloane's room and she saw my face.

"Oh my God," said Sloane a few seconds later.

I walked over and kissed her. "It hurts worse than it looks."

"Did the two of you make up?"

"He forgave me when I told him I bought your dream house."

Sloane smiled, but it was fleeting.

"We need to talk," I said before she could.

"We do."

"Maybe we could ask everyone—" Before I could finish my sentence, my phone rang with the one tone I couldn't ignore. "I have to get this," I said, pulling the cell out of my pocket. Halo followed me out into the hall. "Sorenson."

"Tackle, it's Doc. Where are you?"

"Mass General with Sloane. Halo is here with me."

"Somebody got to Nick. I don't know her condition other than it's pretty bad. I think they may be bringing her to that same hospital."

"Roger that."

"I'll make some calls and confirm it. Wait. You said you're there with Sloane. What's wrong?"

"Something called placenta previa, but the doctor said she and the baby will both be okay."

"Bed rest," he muttered. "I'll call you back in a few."

I didn't need to relay everything Doc had said. Halo heard it. What I did need to do was fill him in on everything that had happened with Nick since he'd left for New York City the last time. I'd just finished when Doc called back.

"She should be arriving any minute. I've got Cowboy on the scene back at her parents' house. Ranger and Diesel will be on the next flight out."

"Copy that."

I leaned up against the wall, dreading having to go in and tell Sloane that I, once again, had to leave her to go check on Nick.

"I'll go deal with Nick," said Halo like he'd just read my mind. "I'll report back when I know her condition."

"Thanks," I said, gripping his shoulder.

"Go take care of my sister."

"Roger that."

"What is it?" Sloane asked when I walked back into the room.

"Halo is taking care of it."

She nodded and turned to her mother. "It's okay if you and Dad want to head home."

"You're sure, *mija*?"

"Positive. I need to sleep so I can come home tomorrow."

"We'll be back in the morning."

Once Ben and Carolina were gone, I sat on the edge of the bed.

"May I?" I held my hand over her belly.

"What?"

"Feel the baby?"

She moved the blanket and sheet away and raised her gown. I rested my hands on her bare skin and closed my eyes, willing our little girl to let me feel her. She didn't disappoint. When I felt her tiny kick, I opened my eyes and looked into Sloane's. "Such a miracle."

"I know," she said, rubbing her stomach and then covering it back up with the blanket.

"You're planning on going to your parents' tomorrow?"

"I think it would be best."

"Why?"

"I know about Nick, Tackle."

"You do? How? Did your dad get a call too?"

"What are you talking about?"

"That's what the call was about earlier. Someone, from Caruso's crew would be my guess, got to her. Beat her up pretty bad. Doc doesn't know her condition but said it's not good. They're bringing her here, actually."

"Oh my God. What about the baby?" she gasped.

"Sloane, I honestly don't believe that you or the baby are in any danger, but I can arrange for more security if it would make you feel more comfortable."

"Not our baby; her, and your, baby."

"What are you talking about? Nick isn't pregnant."

"Tackle, don't lie to me. I saw her. She came to the duplex the morning you left for California."

"What? This isn't making any sense. Nick was in Chicago, not Boston."

"No, she wasn't. She showed up at my place mid-morning. I was expecting my mother, so like an idiot, I opened the door without looking to see who it was." Sloane shifted to her side. "Anyway, she took one look at me and said that she'd come to ask me to let you go so you and she could raise your baby together. After she saw me, she said she figured I would ask her the same thing."

"Nick isn't pregnant."

"Tackle, I saw her."

"So did I. How pregnant did she tell you she was?"

"She didn't need to tell me. She was as big as I am."

"I saw her a few hours after that. She didn't look the slightest bit pregnant."

"You and Nick aren't having a baby?"

"Of course we aren't. Is that why you disappeared on me again?"

"I needed time to think. She was pretty convincing."

"How so?"

"She said she could prove it. She was about to call you, but I slammed the door in her face. I'm telling you, she looked pregnant, Tackle."

"I can't explain why. All I know is that when she landed in California, she didn't."

"What happened when you were there?"

"Nick said she wanted to move back to Boston. I told her I believed it would be dangerous for her to do so. She said she'd made up her mind and that was what she was doing."

"What else?"

"I told her if she did, I wouldn't step in to help her again. Nor would K19."

"I guess she did it anyway."

"She probably thought I was bluffing. I guess it didn't take long for Caruso's crew to find her." I shook my head, wishing she'd just listened and stayed in California.

"He probably thinks it was Nick who got him arrested."

I agreed.

"Check on her," said Sloane.

"Absolutely not. One, I'm not leaving you. Two, your brother is down there, seeing what he can find out. Three, I warned her, and she refused to listen."

"No guilt?"

"More like no regret. Doc told me early on that I needed to separate myself from her, not let her manipulate me. I feel as though that's exactly what she did."

"She didn't get her way, though."

"You're right. She never would've either."

"Tackle, can you do something for me?"

"Of course."

"You said Knox was seeing what he could find out."

"That's right."

"Have him ask about a baby."

Sure, it bothered me that Sloane didn't believe me when I told her Nick wasn't pregnant, but asking for that little bit of reassurance for her, certainly wouldn't hurt me. Instead of texting Halo, I called him and put the phone on speaker.

"Any word?"

"Not yet. They won't let me back there, which isn't a surprise."

"If you're able to talk to anyone, ask if she's pregnant."

"Pregnant?"

"She told Sloane she was."

"Let me guess. Your baby?"

"I saw her a few hours after your sister did, and she didn't look at all pregnant. Sloane said she did."

"Easy enough to shove a pillow under your sweater, I guess."

Sloane rolled her eyes. "Like I wouldn't have known the difference, Knox."

"Aren't there costumes or something that you can wear to make you look pregnant?" he asked.

"I think there are." Sloane's eyes were on mine. "Just ask, though, okay?"

"Roger that."

35

Sloane

I wanted to believe Tackle. And really, it wasn't hard to do so. He wouldn't lie about something that would be so easy to prove otherwise.

It made me feel like a terrible person that I cared whether or not she was pregnant more than if she was going to be okay.

"Sloane, there's something I need to tell you."

My stomach sank.

He leaned forward and caressed my cheek. "It isn't anything bad. At least, I don't think it is."

"What?"

He smiled and kissed me. "I overheard everything you said to Halo earlier."

My cheeks flushed.

"There was one thing in particular that made me think more than the others. You said you didn't know if I'd ever feel the same way about you as you feel about me."

I sighed. "I did say that."

"That's exactly how I felt on the plane ride back from Columbia. I didn't know whether you felt the same way I did, and you wanna know why?"

"Sure."

"Because I never told you how I felt." Tackle brushed my lips with his. "I love you, Sloane."

My eyes filled with tears, and I shook my head.

"Listen to me. I *love* you, Sloane. I have for as long as I can remember."

"You don't have to do this."

"Do what?"

"Feel like you have to say it to me."

"What if I want to say it? What if I want to say it over and over and over until you believe me?"

"I guess I can't stop you."

"You know what?"

I smiled. "What?"

"Other than by eavesdropping, I don't know how you feel about me."

"You heard me."

"I want to hear the words."

This was a lot harder than I'd ever thought it would be. Loving Tackle had been my secret since I was a child. Other than Knox, I hadn't told anyone that I loved him.

"You won't lose part of your soul if you say it, peanut." He smiled and kissed me. "Look, I didn't."

"You can't see your soul to know one way or another."

"That may be true, but I can feel it, and it feels whole."

He shifted down my body and kissed my belly. "I love you too, little peanut. See, it isn't so hard once you practice a few times."

I wove my fingers in his hair and stared into his eyes. "I love you, Landry."

He raised his eyebrows.

I moved his hand to my belly and put mine on top of it. "I love you too, baby Landry."

"Baby Landry? Not baby Sorenson?"

I shook my head. "When I was eleven years old, I decided that whether we had a boy or a girl, our first baby's name would be Landry, just like his or her father."

"You knew then, huh?"

"I think I did. At least I hoped."

We heard a knock at the door. "Come in," I shouted.

"Hey, sorry to interrupt," said my brother, looking sheepishly from Tackle to me. "This is going to be weird."

"You'll get used to it, and if you don't, tough shit."

We all laughed at Tackle's words.

"Have you heard anything?" I asked.

Knox nodded. "They're taking her into surgery."

"Anything else?" Tackle asked.

My brother walked over to the window and looked up at the sky. "I started a shit show."

"What does that mean?"

He turned around to face me. "Her mother was the one to tell me they were taking Nick into the operating room. I asked if the baby was going to be okay."

"You didn't?" I gasped.

"I did."

"And?" asked Tackle.

"There was a lot of yelling."

"Did you get an answer of any kind?"

"Given their shock, I'd say she didn't look pregnant."

My brother looked out the window again. His expression was troubled. "What else, Knox?"

"I also talked to Razor. Word is that someone carried out a hit on Caruso."

"Do they know when?" Tackle asked.

"He thinks within the last hour. He's working on confirmation now."

"I'm sorry to sound less than sympathetic, but why does Caruso's death bother you so much?"

"It doesn't, peanut. I just don't like to talk about stuff like that around the baby."

I smiled and held my hand out to my brother. "Get over here and let me give you a hug."

After Knox left, Tackle insisted on staying at the hospital with me overnight. "If you're on bed rest, so am I," he told me, sitting in what looked like a really uncomfortable chair.

A little while later, when one of the nurses came in to check on me, she told him the recliner in the corner opened to something closer to a bed. He rolled it over so he could still hold my hand when we fell asleep.

The next morning, when my parents arrived, I told them I'd decided to stay at the Chestnut Hill house instead of with them.

"Our house," Tackle said when he heard how I referred to it.

"I'll come over and help, and so will your father."

"I appreciate that, Mom, but it's still being renovated. You might be in the way."

"We're done, except for the exterior," muttered Tackle, stretching his arms over his head.

"You are?"

"My dad had crews working around the clock to finish up what was left of the inside. Pays to own a construction company, I guess."

"Tackle, can I speak with you for a minute?" my father asked.

"Of course."

Both men left the room.

"What's that all about, Mom?"

"Your father wants to talk to Tackle about a job."

"He wants to do construction?"

She rolled her eyes. "He's retiring, and there may be a position with the State Department opening up."

"Oh."

I didn't want to appear ungrateful, but I had no interest in history repeating itself. Tackle knew how I felt, and I hoped he'd at least discuss it with me if he was interested in pursuing it. I hated that it felt as though I was testing him, but I was. If he took the job with State or went back to work full time for K19 and didn't talk it over with me first, we were going to have a problem. There was no way I would agree to live the kind of life my mother had. But what was the alternative? Would I issue him an ultimatum like I guessed my mother had done to my father? If I did, wouldn't I be showing him the same lack of respect I didn't want him to show me?

I thought back to when I drafted my imaginary dating-site listing. Boring homebody, I'd said, but I knew deep down, clipping Tackle's wings would result in neither of us being happy.

When they came back in, I held my breath. Tackle looked stressed, which told me everything I needed to know.

"What do you need at the house?" my mother asked, maybe to break the tension in the room. "We'll go shopping."

Tackle looked at me, and I shrugged. "Food?"

"Sure."

"Let's go, Carolina," said my father. "We'll check with Sloane and Tackle after they've had a chance to get settled and better figure out what they need."

My mother kissed my forehead and rested her hand on my belly. "I love you, *mija*."

After my father kissed me too, they both left and I turned to Tackle.

"Tell me what happened."

"Your father said there's a job opening with State."

"My mom told me. How do you feel about it?"

"I don't want to be away from you and the baby."

I breathed a sigh of relief.

"I told him the only way I'd consider it is if I worked from home."

"Home? What about the travel?"

Tackle's eyes scrunched. "I'd never take anything that involved travel. God, I can't even imagine being away from you and our little girl for a couple of hours, let alone days."

"You're serious, aren't you?"

He studied me. "Of course I am."

"Thank you."

"I don't know why you're thanking me, but you're welcome. You should know my reasons are entirely selfish, though."

"No, they aren't, and it's only one of many reasons I love you."

The door opened, and the doctor I'd seen in the emergency room walked in. "Ready to go home?"

"So ready."

36

Tackle

"What are you doing?" Sloane asked when I lifted her from the car into my arms.

"Carrying you inside."

"Tackle, I can—"

"The doctor was very clear. You have to stay off your feet unless you want to spend the rest of your pregnancy in the hospital."

Instead of arguing, she put her arms around my neck. "I'm heavy."

I laughed. "You're anything but heavy."

"Did you fight back?" she asked, barely touching the area beneath my still-swollen eye.

"Only to try to protect myself."

"Knox had no right."

"We both knew he'd be angry." As I approached the back steps of our house, the door swung open and Halo walked out.

"Want me to take her?"

I tightened my grip on Sloane's body. "I've got you, peanut."

She rested her head on my shoulder as I carried her inside and up the staircase.

"Everything ready?" I asked when I got to the top of the stairs.

"Sure is," Halo answered.

Sloane raised her head when I turned toward the smaller bedroom rather than the master.

"Close your eyes," I whispered.

She looked at her brother, who stood in front of the closed door, and then back at me. "What's going on?"

"Close 'em, Sloane."

When she did, I nodded and Halo opened the door. I carried her inside and set her down in the rocking chair in the room that had been empty when both she and I had last seen it. "Okay, you can open your eyes."

She gasped, taking in the room that her brother had spent last evening and most of this morning decorating. "Oh my God, Knox. It's beautiful," she cried.

"It really is," I said, walking over to pick up the tiny pink football that sat on a shelf and tossing it to him. "You outdid yourself."

"How did you know?" asked Sloane, motioning to the hand-painted lettering on the crib that read, "Landry."

"A little bird told me," he answered with a wink. He walked over to the bedroom door. "Tara, sweetheart? Where are you?"

"I didn't want to intrude," I heard her say from the hallway. When Halo pulled her into the room, I walked over and hugged her.

"Thank you," I murmured.

"You're welcome," she answered before walking over to the rocking chair. "You must be Sloane."

"And you must be Tara. It's so nice to meet you."

Tara knelt down and put her hand on the chair's arm. "I feel like I already know you. Knox talks about you endlessly."

"Oh dear."

"It's all good. I promise."

"Sloane, Tara is an artist," said Halo, running his hand over the name on the crib. "She did this along with the rest you see." Each piece of furniture, the rocker included, was adorned with flowers, vines, even birds.

"It's so beautiful." Sloane looked at me and smiled. "I take it you knew about all this?"

"After the third text asking my opinion, I relinquished all remaining decisions to your brother."

"He does have really good taste." I saw Sloane wink at Tara, who smiled too. "I told him he'd make someone an excellent husband someday. I'm so glad it'll be you."

Tara's cheeks turned pink, and she looked up at Halo. "Me too."

"Got a minute?" he asked me, motioning to the hallway.

"You'll be okay?" I asked Sloane.

"I promise not to get out of the chair. Tara will be my witness."

I followed Halo out and down the stairs.

"What's up?"

"I checked in on Nick before you got here. She's going to be fine. Whoever got to her, broke her arm in a couple of places, and that's why she needed surgery."

"Is there any more information about the hit on Caruso?"

"Negative, and I doubt there will be."

"I warned her," I said as much to myself as to him.

"About that."

I raised my head. "What?"

"Evidently, she's agreed to go back to California."

"Who told you that?"

"Doc told me, but he heard it from Messick."

I remembered seeing something pass between the two of them when he brought her to the house from the airport. "Her and Ranger, huh?"

Halo shrugged. "No idea, but it kinda sounded like it."

"If so, he knows what he's getting into. It's none of my business anymore."

When Halo and I walked back into what I now thought of as Baby Landry's room, Tara was sitting cross-legged on the floor and both women were laughing so hard tears ran down their cheeks.

"I don't think I want to know," said Halo.

"What they're laughing about? Me either."

When she saw me, Sloane held out her hand.

"Need to go lie down?"

"I do. I'm sorry, Tara."

"Don't be. Goodness. All of my best friends are expecting, except for one. The point is, I'm around pregnant women all day, so I get it."

"All day?"

"Tara has a gallery in the city. They spend a lot of time there," said Halo.

"When you're ready, I'd love to paint a mural on that wall." Tara pointed to the one farthest from the front of the house. "I didn't do it now because there will be fumes."

"You've already done so much," said Sloane, yawning when I lifted her into my arms.

"She really wants to do it, sis," said Halo, putting his arm around Tara's shoulders.

"Then, I'd really love it."

"We'll let ourselves out." Halo walked over and kissed Sloane's cheek. "Sorry about your face, dude."

I caught Tara's grimace, and so did he.

"I warned her."

Tara shuddered. "I thought you were exaggerating."

I eased Sloane onto the bed and pulled the blanket we kept at the end of it over her. "Can I get you anything?"

"No, but you can lie beside me."

"Gladly."

I kicked off my shoes and crawled in next to her. "How do you feel?"

"Happy."

I'd expected tired, or even hungry. Happy caught me by surprise. "Me too."

"Tackle, you don't have to take the job with the State Department if you don't want it."

"They might not want me when they see the list of my demands."

"What are they?"

"Let's see. I only have to work when I want to. Unlimited paid time off. A million bucks a year plus bonuses."

She swatted me.

"Ouch. You're a brute just like your brother."

"Be serious. Do you really have a list of demands?"

"I do, but it's short."

"What is it?"

"No travel and I work from home."

She looked skeptical.

"Otherwise, it's a no. I told you this at the hospital."

"I know. I just want you to be happy."

"As happy as you are?"

"Exactly."

"All I need is you beside me to make that happen, Sloane."

***

"How is she doing?" I asked my mom a few days later when she came downstairs and sat next to me at the dining room table.

"Fine. She and Carolina are looking at curtains for the baby's room online." My mom motioned to my computer. "Is this going to be your office?"

"No, I'm setting up something in the back bedroom so I'm closer to Sloane if she needs anything. The furniture should be here today."

"You decided to take the job with State?"

"They agreed to everything I asked for, so I could hardly turn it down."

"Ben mentioned something about you being the resident expert on the Middle East."

I nodded. "As long as I never have to go back there."

My mom rested her head in her hand and had a funny look on her face.

"What?"

"It's so nice to see you so happy."

I couldn't help but smile. "It shows, huh?"

"Oh, yes. Although, I sense something is bothering you."

"There is."

"You wanna talk about it?"

I leaned forward and rested my forearms on the table. "Sloane doesn't want to talk about marriage until after Landry's born."

"I still can't believe that's the name the two of you chose. I absolutely love it. But back to your dilemma. Part of Sloane still believes you're only with her because of the baby."

"What about all this?" I waved my arm around the house that we'd made into our home.

"What is obvious to you may not be obvious to a young woman who not only hasn't been in a real relationship before but is also dealing with pregnancy hormones."

"What should I do?"

"Make her believe."

"How?" I put my head in my hands. "I'm so bad at this shit."

"First of all, don't ever let her hear you refer to romance as shit. Next, win her over, my son."

"How?" I repeated.

"No one knows Sloane the way you do. You'll figure it out."

37

Sloane

I knew something was up the minute Tackle came into the bedroom and closed the door behind him. He walked over to the bed, sat beside me, and pulled a familiar-looking piece of silk out of his pocket. The heat emanating from him kept me silent as he covered my eyes.

He unfastened the buttons on the blouse I was wearing. I gasped when he pulled the cups of my bra down and took one of my nipples into his mouth.

"I need you naked, Sloane."

I nodded but still didn't speak even when I felt his hands on the waistband of my sweatpants. I lifted my bottom as he removed them along with my panties.

"Now this," he said, unfastening my bra. When it was off and he put his hand on the back of my neck and kissed me, I whimpered with need.

"Tell me, Sloane, what are the rules when you're naked?"

"Whatever you tell me to do, I do."

"Mmm, that's right. What's the other rule?"

I could barely speak with how badly I wanted him. "Tell the truth."

"You remember. That makes me very happy."

"Tackle, please."

"Shh."

When I reached out to touch him, he grabbed my hand and licked my palm.

"I'm going to ask you another question, Sloane. If you tell me the truth, you'll get a reward."

My body started to writhe. "Okay," I whined.

"Do you believe the only reason I want to marry you is because of the baby?"

"Tackle—"

He pinched my nipple, and I almost came off the bed. "Answer, peanut. The truth please."

I rested my head against the pillow. I knew why he was doing this. He wanted answers, and I wanted his hands, lips, tongue, and cock. He would win this game, and he knew it.

"Yes."

"Another honest answer, do you know how hard that makes me?"

I felt his fingers between my legs, spreading my folds; I opened for him.

"I want you to know that I spoke with Dr. Phillips. Everything I'm going to do to your body today is perfectly safe. It will not harm you or the baby."

When he pinched my clit, I cried out. When I felt his tongue soothe the hardened nub, I orgasmed. He didn't stop, though. Instead, he brought me right back to the brink.

"Next question. Do you believe me when I tell you I love you?"

"Y-y-yes."

"Good girl."

He moved, and the next thing I felt were his hands and lips on my breasts. I wove my fingers in his hair.

"Keep still, Sloane," he said when I tried to angle the lower half of my body closer to him. "Next question. Do you love me?"

"Yes."

"How much?"

"Oh, God, Tackle," I moaned when I felt his fingers back between my legs.

"That isn't an answer."

"I love you so much."

"Enough to know that you want to spend the rest of your life with me?"

"Tackle..."

He moved away so no part of his body was touching mine. "Answer me, Sloane."

"Yes."

"Yes, what?"

"Yes, I love you enough to spend the rest of my life with you."

"You've been very honest. That means the world to me." His tongue was back on my clit in an instant, bringing me to yet another orgasm.

As my breathing slowed, I waited for his next question. Instead, I felt the shift of the bed when he stood. "Tackle?"

"I'm right here." I heard the rustling of clothes and then his hands removed the silk covering my eyes. "With this, you have a choice," he said, kneeling at the side of the bed.

He took my left hand in his and slid a ring on my finger. "Sloane, will you marry me?"

My eyes filled with tears, and I nodded.

"I need to hear the words."

"I will marry you, Tackle."

He stood, walked around the bed, and lay naked beside me. I turned my body toward his, and we kissed.

"I love you, Sloane."

"I love you, Landry."

He raised a brow.

"It is your name."

He laughed. "As long as you love me, I don't really care what you call me."

There were many things I was tempted to say, but he'd just proposed and I'd accepted. I didn't want to make a joke of something I'd dreamed about my entire life.

I leaned forward and kissed him as tears ran down my cheeks. He pulled back and looked into my eyes. "I want you to be my wife, Sloane. I want it so much, it hurts, and that's the part I want you to know. I understand we need to wait, since you're on bed rest, but know that if I could, I'd marry you today."

"What about Thursday?"

"Thursday?"

"There's a three-day waiting period to get the marriage license in Massachusetts."

"Is that right?"

"I doubt the justice of the peace would be busy on a weekday."

Tackle smiled. "Unlikely."

"You'd probably want to call just to make sure."

"You've thought about this?"

"No, Tackle, I've dreamed about this—my whole life."

Epilogue

Tackle

On the twentieth day of August, Landry Carolina Alice Sorenson made her debut. Sloane and I decided we didn't want anyone in the delivery room with us other than the doctors and nurses, much to both our mothers' dismay.

Three hours after her water broke, Sloane grasped my hand with hers as we watched our baby girl take her first breaths.

I cried unashamedly when the doctor placed Landry on Sloane's chest, and she looked first at her mother and then at me.

"She looks like you," said Sloane.

I shook my head. "She looks like you, and she's perfect."

***

A little less than two years later, Landry's baby brother joined our family. Sloane told me that since she'd chosen the name for our precocious and precious little girl, she wanted me to choose the name for our boy.

He was two weeks old when I came to Sloane with the name I'd finally decided on. It hadn't been hard to come up with, only the order was.

"Bodhi Nils Benjamin Sorenson."

"I love it," said Sloane, kissing our baby boy's head, Landry's cheek, and then my lips.

Keep reading for a sneak peek
at the next book in the
K19 Security Solutions Series—
ONYX!

1

Onyx

I couldn't remember the last time I spent Thanksgiving with my entire family. With five brothers and three sisters, all of whom were married with kids, my parents' place, while large enough to raise us all in, was still a madhouse.

Fortunately, it was warm enough today in Paso Robles, located just inland on the Central Coast of California, that we could spend the day outdoors.

"What can I get you?" my sister Erlinda asked, coming over to where I sat chatting with my oldest brother, Carlos. "Would you like another glass of wine?"

I looked at my half-full glass. "I'm good."

When she walked away, Carlos cleared his throat. "Ahem."

"You can get your own," Erlinda said over her shoulder.

I watched the kids—none of whom I recognized—as they ran around the large lawn on the side of the house. When we were their age, there didn't seem to be much time for playing. Even on holidays, there was work to do in the vineyards that sat on our parents' property but were leased by my cousins, the Avilas, for their Los Caballeros Winery.

"How was the harvest this year?" I asked Carlos, more to be polite than because I cared. I'd never had any interest in growing grapes or making wine.

From the time I was a small boy, all I'd wanted to do was become a pilot. I followed a path from the Navy's ROTC program, into college, active duty, Officer Candidate School, and finally into pilot training. Along with flying F/A-18 Hornets, I cross-trained in intelligence.

That's what led me to go work for K19 Security Solutions, a firm founded by four of the CIA's best operatives and agents. Hell, they were the world's best.

It was my job with K19 that took me to South America that fateful day when my life irrevocably changed. I'd come as close to dying as any man ever had when I was shot at point-blank range while flying an aircraft that subsequently crashed.

Sure, everyone said it was a miracle I was alive, but I wasn't, not fully. I'd lost two parts of myself the minute the shot was fired.

First, my career as a pilot came to an end. The injuries I suffered would never heal enough for me to fly again.

Second, the organ responsible for pumping blood throughout my body had turned black as coal when Corazón—the woman whose very code name meant heart—fired the gun intending to kill me.

In the split second when I realized what was about to happen, my eyes met hers and I said what I thought would be my last words, "I love you, Corazón."

She'd laughed and pulled the trigger anyway.

That was one year ago today, and in that time, I'd spent a month in a coma and four months learning to walk again. Learning to love again was something I'd never be able to do. I didn't want to.

"Montano?" I heard my mother call my name.

"Someone actually expects you to get off your ass?" Carlos muttered, but I knew he was joking. He'd been there, along with my closest friend, Monk, through weeks of agonizing rehab when I was forced to work my body harder than I ever had.

"There's someone here to see you," she added.

I rounded the corner of the yard to the front of the house and gripped the front porch's railing when I saw the ghost that stood before me. "*Corazón?*"

About the Author

USA Today and Amazon Top 15 Bestselling Author Heather Slade writes shamelessly sexy, edge-of-your seat romantic suspense.

She gave herself the gift of writing a book for her own birthday one year. Forty-plus books later (and counting), she's having the time of her life.

The women Slade writes are self-confident, strong, with wills of their own, and hearts as big as the Colorado sky. The men are sublimely sexy, seductive alphas who rise to the challenge of capturing the sweet soul of a woman whose heart they'll hold in the palm of their hand forever. Add in a couple of neck-snapping twists and turns, a page-turning mystery, and a swoon-worthy HEA, and you'll be holding one of her books in your hands.

She loves to hear from my readers. You can contact her at heather@heatherslade.com

To keep up with her latest news and releases, please visit her website at www.heatherslade.com to sign up for her newsletter.

MORE FROM AUTHOR HEATHER SLADE

BUTLER RANCH

Kade's Worth

Brodie

Maddox

Naughton

Mercer

Kade

Christmas at Butler Ranch

WICKED WINEMAKERS' BALL

Coming soon:

Brix

Ridge

Press

K19 SECURITY SOLUTIONS

Razor

Gunner

Mistletoe

Mantis

Dutch

Striker

Monk

Halo

Tackle

Onyx

K19 SHADOW OPERATIONS

Code Name: Ranger

Coming soon:

Code Name: Diesel

Code Name: Wasp

Code Name: Cowboy

THE ROYAL AGENTS OF MI6

The Duke and the Assassin

The Lord and the Spy

The Commoner and the Correspondent

The Rancher and the Lady

THE INVINCIBLES

Decked

Undercover Agent

Edged

Grinded

Riled

Handled

Smoked

Bucked

Irished

Sainted

Coming soon:

Hammered

Ripped

COWBOYS OF CRESTED BUTTE

A Cowboy Falls

A Cowboy's Dance

A Cowboy's Kiss

A Cowboy Stays

A Cowboy Wins